App[le Pie]

A Freshly Baked Cozy Mystery

by
Kathleen Suzette

Books by Kathleen Suzette:

A Rainey Daye Cozy Mystery Series

A Pumpkin Hollow Mystery Series

Candy Coated Murder
A Pumpkin Hollow Mystery, book 1
Murderously Sweet
A Pumpkin Hollow Mystery, book 2
Chocolate Covered Murder
A Pumpkin Hollow Mystery, book 3
Death and Sweets
A Pumpkin Hollow Mystery, book 4
Sugared Demise
A Pumpkin Hollow Mystery, book 5
Confectionately Dead
A Pumpkin Hollow Mystery, book 6
Hard Candy and a Killer
A Pumpkin Hollow Mystery, book 7
Candy Kisses and a Killer
A Pumpkin Hollow Mystery, book 8
Terminal Taffy
A Pumpkin Hollow Mystery, book 9
Fudgy Fatality
A Pumpkin Hollow Mystery, book 10
Truffled Murder
A Pumpkin Hollow Mystery, book 11
Caramel Murder
A Pumpkin Hollow Mystery, book 12
Peppermint Fudge Killer
A Pumpkin Hollow Mystery, book 13
Chocolate Heart Killer
A Pumpkin Hollow Mystery, book 14

A Freshly Baked Cozy Mystery Series
Apple Pie A La Murder,
A Freshly Baked Cozy Mystery, Book 1
Trick or Treat and Murder,
A Freshly Baked Cozy Mystery, Book 2
Thankfully Dead
A Freshly Baked Cozy Mystery, Book 3
Candy Cane Killer
A Freshly Baked Cozy Mystery, Book 4
Ice Cold Murder
A Freshly Baked Cozy Mystery, Book 5
Love is Murder
A Freshly Baked Cozy Mystery, Book 6
Strawberry Surprise Killer
A Freshly Baked Cozy Mystery, Book 7
Plum Dead
A Freshly Baked Cozy Mystery, book 8
A Gracie Williams Mystery Series
Pushing Up Daisies in Arizona,
A Gracie Williams Mystery, Book 1
Kicked the Bucket in Arizona,
A Gracie Williams Mystery, Book 2

A Home Economics Mystery Series
Appliqued to Death
A Home Economics Mystery, book 1

Table of Contents

Chapter One

"It'll be the death of you if you can't convince him to change," Lucy said, nodding. "I know it's driving you crazy. He has no idea what he's doing, and you have the answer to his problems."

"Tell me about it," I said, rolling out the piecrust to an even thickness.

She was right. I knew better than to try another slice of Henry Hoffer's pies. The cherry pie resembled cherry flavored gelatin in a crust. His restaurant was called Henry's Home Cooking Restaurant, but he wasn't fooling anyone with the pies. They were store-bought, and not even a name brand.

"Tell Henry you want to bake pies to sell at his restaurant. The pies alone will double his business," Lucy said, relaxing at my kitchen table. A cup of coffee was in her hand, and she had slipped her shoes off under the table.

"I don't know about that," I replied as I ran a hand over the piecrust dough. It was beautiful.

"Henry would be lucky to have your pies to sell," she encouraged me. "Everyone loves your pies."

Peeled and sliced Granny Smith apples were in a bowl on the counter beside me, marinating in sugar and cinnamon, their juices pooling in the bottom of the bowl. My apple pies were as American as you could get.

"I'm glad you have confidence in my pies," I said. I was making the pie, but I still wasn't convinced Henry would agree to do business with me. That Henry could be stubborn.

I brushed the top of the pie with a butter and cinnamon sugar glaze and finished crimping the crust. Then I slid it into the preheated oven and closed the door, anticipating the wonderful apple cinnamon smell that was about to fill my house. It was one of the signature scents of fall. I had been baking a pie every day for years. Don't judge. There was a method to my madness. Or at least, there was a reason for it.

I had grown up in Alabama, and my grandmama was the best pie baker in the county. She made a fresh pie every day. It was fortunate for me that she lived right next door. By the time I was fourteen, I could make a piecrust so flaky it would make you cry.

"Allie, I think you're too modest about your baking talents," Lucy said, taking a sip of her coffee. A thin blue headband held her short blond hair back.

I chuckled. "Modesty isn't my problem," I said. "I just don't know if I really want to do this."

When I moved away to college, I gave up the pursuit of pie baking for the pursuit of men, namely one Thaddeus McSwain, from Maine. We married and lived a happy life, having two children and a cute little house with a white picket fence in a small town. Our son was named after my husband, and our daughter, Jennifer.

But a drunk driver had cut my husband's life short. My life and my children's lives would never be the same. I began baking a pie every day shortly after his death. The comfort of something as familiar as buttery pastry dough and marinating fruit helped me to heal. It was therapy.

My cat Dixie rubbed up against my leg and purred loudly.

"Hey guy, how are you?" I murmured as I squatted beside him and rubbed his head. Dixie was all black with yellow-green eyes, and like most cats, he seemed to be able to take or leave my companionship. I straightened up and set a timer for the pie.

"You're a marvel, Allie," Lucy said, picking up her cup of coffee and taking another sip. "There's no one in Sandy Harbor that bakes as well as you do."

I smiled. "Why, thank you, Lucy. It makes me happy that people appreciate my baking."

"This little endeavor is going to be a roaring success. I'm glad I thought of it," she said, stirring her coffee. Lucy was six years older than me, and sometimes she dyed her short blond hair wild colors. She's the best friend I've ever had.

"You know I have a blog on grief to write, and I don't have the time nor the inclination to start a side business," I protested.

"But you're baking a pie every day as it is. You may as well get paid for it. Maybe you'll make enough money to help pay off the kids' college loans."

She was right. I was baking a pie every day. And when the holidays rolled around, it seemed there was always someone asking me to bake something for them. I wasn't sure I could handle baking more than a couple of pies a day regularly, but

Sandy Harbor, Maine, was a small town. How many pies could Henry sell? If he even agreed to it.

Chapter Two

IT WAS ALMOST FIVE in the evening by the time the pie had cooled enough for me to take to Henry. I didn't want it to cool off completely because it was best while still warm. Add a scoop of vanilla ice cream, and you had a slice of heaven on a plate.

I put the pie in one of my grandmama's ceramic pie keepers, and I hoped Henry would appreciate all the gaily painted dancing apples on it. After all, presentation is everything.

Ralph Henderson was weeding one of the garden planters in front of the restaurant when I got there. I nodded at him and smiled as I passed. "Hello, Ralph," I sang.

Ralph glanced at me, snorted, and turned back to his work, his large square body bent over the dark soil. I shook my head, but kept to myself and pushed open the restaurant door. Ralph was a quiet one that kept to himself, so leaving him to his business was the least I could do.

Henry's Home Cooking Restaurant was a quiet, out of the way place that served dependable, if a bit dull, fare. Most of the time it was tasty, except for his pies, of course.

The smell of pine cleaner hit my nose as I headed toward the back of the restaurant. The dinner crowd was starting to trickle in, and Henry had been cleaning after the lunch rush. But that's what Henry always did. There was one thing you could always count on at Henry's. The place would be immaculately clean. Henry was a germaphobe.

"Hello, Eileen, is Henry around?" I asked the waitress.

Eileen was popping her gum, bent over a table scrubbing off dried food. She looked at me without stopping what she was doing. "Ayuh, he's in the back," she said and pointed toward the open doorway that led to the backroom. She flipped her long black hair over her shoulder and turned back to her work.

"Thanks, Eileen," I said with a smile and a nod. As I headed back, I wished I had taken an extra second to look at my hair in the mirror. I had thrown it up into a messy bun, but my hair was thick and curly, and I could sense it starting to escape. I was a redhead. Natural, of course.

"Charles," I nodded as I passed the cook.

Charles Allen, head cook at Henry's Home Cooking Restaurant, stopped stirring whatever it was in the huge silver-colored pot on the stove and stared at me. He wiped a hand across his brow, but never took his eyes off me. I was trespassing. He didn't say a word though, and I continued on my mission.

The door to Henry's office was at the end of the hallway, and the door was open. I stopped in the doorway and peered in. A half sheet of plywood was attached to the wall with brackets and served as a desk. It must have set Henry back twenty dollars. Henry was pouring over a ledger with tiny cursive writing on the pages, and a neatly stacked pile of papers sat on the desk. Henry didn't look up when I entered. His bald spot was expanding, and his blond stringy hair could use a good combing. He gripped a yellow number two pencil in one hand.

Come into the computer age, Henry.

I cleared my throat.

Henry jumped as if stung by a bee. "What? What do you want?" he asked, staring at me wide-eyed.

I smiled bigger. "Henry, I have a proposition for you," I said, holding the pie keeper in front of myself. "I don't want to insult you, but your pies are disgusting. Why don't we go into business together? I make the best pies in the county, thanks to my grandmama's training. I brought a sample for you to try. I'm sure you'll be delighted with it." Lucy had said to be confident, and it was oozing out of my pores now.

I know it sounded harsh, calling his pies disgusting, but they were, and you have to know Henry. He appreciated directness.

He frowned. "I don't want none of your pies," he said. "Get out."

See? What did I tell you?

"Henry, try my apple pie while it's still warm. I guarantee you it's the best you've ever tasted." I smiled for all I was worth. A Southern woman knows how to charm.

"Get out of my restaurant unless you're here to buy something," he said through gritted teeth. His fingers tightened around the pencil.

"Now, Henry, I've known you for twenty years. You can't even bake a pie. You buy them at Shaw's Market. Everyone hates your desserts. Think of all the money we could make if we joined forces to bring the people of Sandy Harbor delicious desserts."

"I said, get out!" Henry exclaimed, narrowing his eyes at me.

"I just want you to try it," I coaxed. "I guarantee you it's the best apple pie you've ever eaten."

"Out!" he said, pointing the pencil at the doorway. "Now! Or I'll call Sam Bailey."

Sam Bailey was the police chief, and he moved slower than a turtle jogging through peanut butter, so I had no worries there.

"Henry, you're being unreasonable!" I exclaimed.

"I'll show you unreasonable. Get out of my office!"

"Listen, Henry, I'll leave. Right now. If you promise to at least try my pie. We can work out the details later."

Henry stared at me, his face turning red.

He sighed. "Fine, I'll try your pie," he relented. "But the dinner rush is about to begin, and I need to concentrate. I can't have people popping in here whenever they want."

I smiled. That was more like it. "Promise to taste it while it's still warm? It won't be the same once it's cold."

He breathed out through his mouth and nodded his head without saying anything more.

"Great, I'll talk to you later. Oh, and I need that pie keeper back. It was my grandmama's," I said before exiting his office. I passed Charles on my way out. He stopped stirring again and stared at me.

I shook my head and kept moving. I don't know why people have to be so difficult. It was a free pie, for goodness sake.

Chapter Three

I woke up bright and early the next morning while it was still dark. Wrapping my pink fuzzy robe around me, I stumbled to the coffeemaker and poured water into the machine. As I ground up fresh French Vanilla coffee beans, I inhaled the lovely, rich aroma and yawned.

I was a runner in training for a marathon. Fall running was tough. But winter running was worse. All my body wanted to do was stay nice and warm in my cozy flannel pajamas and hunker down for the rest of the increasingly colder days. My late husband had laughed at me every morning that first winter we moved to Maine. I wasn't a runner back then, but the cold Northern winter had caught me by surprise. I cried almost every time I had to go outside and start my car. But people adjust, and I finally did.

When Thaddeus died nearly eight years ago, my world had crumbled. We would have easily made it to sixty years of marriage. We rarely argued, and when we did, we somehow managed to find some sort of common ground. That, or he gave in. Either way, we got along famously. Being married was all I had ever dreamed of as a little girl. And then it was gone.

I poured a cup of coffee and swallowed back the tears. The anniversary of his death was October ninth. I would wait until then to lose control. And after I cried, I would pull myself together and move forward like I always did.

Ten minutes later, I had my running shoes and cold weather gear on. I grabbed a water bottle and headed out. Driving to the running trail, I passed by Henry's restaurant and decided to stop in when I saw Henry's car parked in the back. He served a great scrambled egg and bacon breakfast. Simple, yet tasty. I decided I needed some protein in my stomach so I wouldn't run out of steam. I made a mental note to teach Henry how to make real Southern biscuits and gravy as I pulled into the parking lot. Biscuits and gravy would make a great addition to his menu and couldn't be beaten on a cold morning.

The restaurant wasn't open yet, so I headed to the back where I had seen Henry's car parked. He had better have tried my pie while it was still warm; I thought as I knocked on the back door. I waited in the cold and bounced up and down on my toes to keep warm. There was no answer, and when I knocked a second time, the back door creaked, slowly swinging open an inch. Huh. Maybe Henry was going back and forth through the back door this morning and hadn't shut it tightly behind himself.

"Henry?" I called out. I waited for an answer, but none came. Would it be rude for me to just walk in? Maybe he was in the bathroom and couldn't hear me. I stabilized the door with one hand and knocked harder. Henry was so cranky, I didn't want him to see me and call the cops for breaking and entering. I glanced at my phone, wishing he would answer me. The coffee had finally kicked in, and I was ready to go for a run.

"Henry?" I called out again. A cold fall breeze was blowing, and I shivered in spite of my insulated jacket.

I pushed the door open a little wider. The back door opened onto the kitchen, and I took two steps inside. "Henry?" I called out again. "Hello!"

Where could he be?

I took two more steps inside, straining my ears for any sound, but it was deathly quiet. I called to him again.

I sighed. And then I saw him. Henry was lying in a pool of blood in front of the wide stainless steel double-door refrigerator. I sucked air in, hard. Had he fallen and cracked his head open? Nope. The steak knife plunged into his chest ruled that out.

I screamed.

"What's going on?" someone asked from behind me. I jumped and screamed again, spinning around.

Charles Allen, Henry's cook, came up behind me, and when he caught sight of Henry, he stopped, mouth open, staring at Henry. "Oh. Wow."

I looked at him, eyes wide, and screamed again.

"Can you stop doing that?" he asked, sounding irritated. He took a step back. His face had gone pale, and one puffy hand rubbed his chin.

I stared at him in silence for a few seconds and then looked at Henry again. "We better call the police," I squeaked.

"Yeah," he said, but neither of us moved. I had never seen a murder victim before. Then I noticed my pie, still in my grandmama's ceramic pie keeper, smashed on the floor beside Henry. Had someone fought him over my pie? That seemed harsh. I would have made another one. I swallowed back the lump forming in my throat. I loved that pie keeper.

"Okay, I'm going to call the police now," Charles said, but he stayed rooted in place.

"Yeah, you do that," I said without looking at him. I wanted to look away, but I couldn't. There was so much blood.

Finally, Charles moved over to the phone on the wall and picked it up. His hands trembled as he dialed. After a few moments, he spoke slowly, his voice quivering as he answered the 911 operator's questions. I looked back at Henry. One arm was across his stomach while the other was out to his side. Wait. *Did he just move his arm?* My eyes must be playing tricks on me, I thought.

Charles placed the telephone receiver against his chest. "They want us to check for a pulse."

"What?" I asked, my head whipping around toward him. "Uh uh. No way." I shook my head at him. Henry was dead. I didn't need to touch him to figure that out.

"Do it!" he hissed at me.

I shook my head. He was on his own with that one. He sighed loudly and then spoke back into the receiver. "Yeah, he's gone." After a few more questions, he hung up the phone.

"You should have checked," he said, not taking his eyes off Henry.

"You should have," I said, looking away from Henry. "I can't stay here. I can't look at him." My head was swimming, and I needed air. I left through the back door and hoped the police showed up soon.

Charles followed me, looking a little green around the gills. I imagined I looked the same way.

"This is terrible," I said, hearing sirens in the distance. "Maybe we should go around the front so the paramedics see us?"

Charles nodded and followed me to the front of the restaurant. We stood near the planter that the gardener had been working on the previous evening. A gardening hoe and some potted mums still sat along the edge. The flowers were in yellow and orange hues. Perfect fall colors. I sighed. Henry would never see another fall. I didn't know Henry very well, and I wondered if he was married. I couldn't remember hearing that he was.

"Was he married?" I asked Charles.

"Huh? Oh, yeah. He married a gal from Chicago three years ago."

"Oh. That's sad." They were practically newlyweds. That made it worse somehow. I thought of all the emotions his wife was soon to go through, and I felt tears spring to my eyes. I blinked them back and looked toward the sound of the sirens.

Chapter Four

A cold shiver went through my body. Seeing Henry dead on his kitchen floor was a horrible sight. Sandy Harbor was a small town, and I couldn't believe anyone local would murder Henry Hoffer. Perhaps a stranger passing through town had done it. The I-95 ran along the edge of town. It would be easy enough for someone to pull off the highway and murder Henry. Maybe they were looking for someone to rob. Henry might have worked late, and the killer, seeing a light still on at the restaurant and only Henry's car in the parking lot, decided it would be an easy take. Then things might have gone from bad to worse, and Henry had ended up dead. As cantankerous as Henry was, it wasn't hard to imagine.

Three police cars pulled up to the front of the restaurant, followed by an ambulance and a black unmarked police car. I hugged myself. All I wanted was to go home and go to bed. Forget about running. Forget about everything. The shock of seeing Henry dead had sucked all the energy right out of me.

Officer Yancey Tucker got out of the first police car. George Feeney and Stuart South were in the others.

"Allie, Charles," Yancey said, nodding first at me, and then Charles.

"Yancey, Henry Hoffer was murdered," I whispered.

His eyes went wide. "Where's he at?"

"Around back in the kitchen," Charles said. "I got a key to the front door, though. We can go in this way, it's faster." He produced a large ring of keys from his front pocket and stuck one in the front door lock.

A tall man in a dark suit stepped out of the unmarked car after finishing a conversation on his cell phone. Suit wearing was rare in these parts, and I had never seen him before. He had black hair and a serious look on his face, and he walked straight toward me.

"I'm Detective Blanchard," he said and stuck his hand out.

"Pleased to meet you," I said, and noticed my voice sounded weak. I cleared my throat, smiled at him, and shook his hand, but he didn't offer me any pleasantries.

"Can I get your name?" he asked, sounding business-like.

I nodded. "Allie McSwain. I didn't know Sandy Harbor had a detective," I said. I was puzzled. Where had he come from? Sandy Harbor had a population of less than twenty thousand, and everyone knew everyone. The detective was a stranger here.

Detective Blanchard glanced at me and then looked in the direction the others had gone.

"Did you find the body?" he asked without explaining where he had come from.

I nodded. "Yes." Something about this man made me nervous.

"Let's go into the restaurant, shall we? I have some questions for you," he said, motioning toward the front door.

Detective Blanchard moved ahead of me and opened the door, allowing me to enter first. I could still smell pine cleaner from the night before, and now, lemon furniture polish, in the air. Henry must have stayed late to clean.

We followed the others back into the kitchen. I would rather not have gone back in there, so I hung out by the kitchen door and looked at my feet.

"Ayup, he's dead all right," Yancey announced.

The back door swung open, and we all turned to look. Martha Newberry appeared, and when she saw Henry on the floor with a knife in his chest, she gasped.

"Oh, dear. Oh, dear," she said, looking from Henry to the policemen. She clutched her pink handbag to her chest and made a low sound in her throat. After a moment, she began to sway on her feet as she looked at Henry.

"Mrs. Newberry, perhaps you might not want to come in here right now," George Feeney said and stepped over the body to take her arm.

"Why, I was just stopping by to help Henry clean this morning. He called last night and said I didn't need to come by. Said he could handle it. But I felt bad about leaving him to do it, so I stopped by to see if he needed any help after all. Oh, dear," she said again, her face crinkled up in shock. Martha was elderly, at least in her late seventies, with blue-tinted curly hair and pink rouged cheeks.

Poor Martha went pale. I doubted she had ever seen anything like this. She picked up work from Henry a couple of days a week, helping him to keep the germs at bay. She was a widow without any children, and I thought she was probably lonely all on her own, and the work was a help with that, as well as financially.

"Why don't we go into the dining room?" George suggested.

"Yes, of course," she said. "I was just... oh, I don't know. I seem to be a bit addled at the moment, forgive me."

"That's quite all right," he said and steered her toward the kitchen door where I was leaning. As Martha passed the kitchen counter, she reached out for a pink covered Pyrex dish that sat there.

"Oh, this will ruin," she said, picking it up and taking it to the refrigerator. She averted her gaze from Henry's body and slipped the dish inside. Poor thing. Whatever was in that dish was already ruined, having sat out on the counter all night. She wasn't thinking straight.

George led her to the dining room, patting her on the shoulder. Martha was too frail to be working a job. It was a shame she felt she needed to.

"I would like to speak with the two of you," the detective said, motioning toward Charles and me, and he led us to the dining room.

I glanced over at Charles. He was still wide-eyed and pale. I took a deep breath. I didn't feel like conversation, and apparently neither did Charles. We followed the detective back to the dining room. George and Martha sat at a corner table at the far end of the room, and he got up to fetch her a glass of water.

The detective motioned to a booth and nodded at me. I swallowed hard.

"Charles, I'll speak to you in a moment. We'd like some privacy," he said when Charles looked like he wanted to take a seat beside me.

"Oh. Okay, sure," he said and walked off. He busied himself straightening papers around the cash register, but his eyes were on the detective and me.

The detective began by taking my personal information and making notes. "Ms. McSwain, what is it you do for a living?" Detective Blanchard asked. He had brilliant blue eyes, and he looked at me very intensely.

I smiled at him. "I'm a blogger."

"What do you blog about?" he asked.

I felt my smile tighten. Why was it still so hard for me to tell someone that the man I had loved more than life itself had died? "Grief."

"Grief?" he asked, eyebrows twitching.

My smile tightened more. "My husband passed away several years ago, and to help me get through it, I began writing a blog on grief."

His eyebrows furrowed, but he didn't say anything else.

"I find it therapeutic, and other people seem to find it helps them with their own grief." I clenched my teeth. Why did I always feel the need to explain myself? Shouldn't the fact that I had lost and grieved be enough? And why was this oaf seemingly confused by that?

"Yes, of course," he said, and scribbled a note in his notebook. His handwriting was terrible, so I couldn't make out what it said. I began to squirm a little. Why did he feel like he needed to keep notes on what I was saying when it had nothing to do with Henry's murder?

"Ms. McSwain, how is it that you find yourself here at the restaurant at 5:00 AM? It doesn't open up until six, correct?" he asked, not looking up at me.

I swallowed. "Well, I had made Henry a pie, and I wanted to stop by on my way to the running trail to ask him how he liked it."

"Oh?" he said, looking at me now. "Were you and Henry, friends?"

"What? No. I was a customer. You know, it's a small town where everyone knows everyone. My friend Lucy suggested I approach Henry and ask him if he would like me to bake pies for his restaurant." Darn that Lucy. If she hadn't insisted, I wouldn't have discovered Henry's body, and I wouldn't have to deal with this detective now.

"I see. A business venture, then?" He scribbled again.

"Yes. A business venture." I suddenly felt like a third grader that had found herself unfairly sent to the principal's office.

"And would that be your pie smashed on the floor next to the murder victim?" He looked me in the eye on this question.

I forced myself to smile. "Yes, it would be. People usually have a more positive reaction to my pies." I laughed, trying to lighten the mood, but got only a blank stare in return from the detective.

He looked at me for what seemed a long time before he continued. I made a mental note that the detective wasn't much on humor.

"And where were you last night?"

My mouth dropped open, and I quickly shut it again. Why was he asking me this question? "I was home. I watched some television and went to bed around nine. I always get up early to run," I said, feeling like I had to explain the early bedtime. After all, I might have been middle-aged, or nearly middle-aged, but I wasn't dead yet. I had a reason for it.

"I see," he said and scribbled in the notebook again.

"A lot of people run," I added lamely.

He looked at me and nodded. "Is there anything you would like to add, Ms. McSwain? Anything that you feel would be of help?"

Yes, how about I didn't do it! What I actually said was, "I can't think of anything else."

"Great, I'm sure we'll be in touch. You can go now."

I looked at him for a minute, and he looked back at me passively. I quickly got to my feet, and I gave Charles a wide-eyed look as I passed him. The detective called him over. Charles looked nervous, and he had a right to be. I felt like I had been probed by a space alien. Surely that detective couldn't suspect someone like me, could he? I had never even had a traffic ticket.

Chapter Five

I didn't go home after speaking to the detective as I had planned. Instead, I drove over to a little corner coffee shop that served the strongest coffee in the state. While waiting in line, I called my friend Lucy.

Just before it switched over to voicemail, she picked up. "Huh?" she mumbled.

"Lucy," I whispered. I got to the front of the line and ordered a vanilla latte from the young woman at the register.

"Huh?" Lucy repeated.

"Ya want that with whipped cream?" the woman asked.

"Yes. Lots. And lots of vanilla syrup and milk," I answered. I needed the caffeine that was in the nearly thick as mud coffee, but I also needed it to be palatable. And right now, I was stressed, and the sugar from the syrup and whipped cream would help settle my nerves.

"What's going on?" Lucy asked, sounding a little more awake now.

"Lucy, I need you to meet me down at the Cup and Bean coffee shop. Now," I whispered into the phone. I looked over my shoulder to make sure no one was eavesdropping. There were about a dozen other customers in the shop, and they all seemed absorbed in their own lives.

"Why? I'm still in bed," Lucy said and yawned. "What time is it, anyway?"

"Lucy, this is important. I need you. Right now," I whispered into the phone.

She must have heard the fear in my voice because she sounded more awake now. "Cup and Bean? I'll be right there."

"Three ninety-five," the woman behind the counter said, ringing up my drink.

I smiled at her and ended the phone call with Lucy without saying anything more to her. She would be here. She always was. I smiled at the woman and dug in my purse for my debit card. Where was that thing? I searched my wallet and then the pockets in my purse. I glanced at the woman and smiled. "I've got it right here. Somewhere."

She gave me a terse smile back as two more customers got in line behind me.

I dug down among the random receipts, gum, and breath mints and glanced over my shoulder, giving the people behind me an apologetic smile. Finally, I found it at the very bottom of my purse and handed it to the cashier.

After she ran it through the machine, I grabbed my drink and found a small table in the corner. I nervously looked at Facebook on my phone while I waited for Lucy.

My daughter Jennifer had posted several pictures of herself at a party. I would have to speak to her about that. She needed to be studying, not enjoying college life. My aunt Mary posted pictures of her roses, and my mother posted a recipe. I sighed. I was addicted to Facebook, even though there wasn't much of anything interesting on there.

I stirred my latte and glanced at the clock on the wall. It had been ten minutes since I had called Lucy. I took a sip of my drink and grimaced at the bite of the coffee. It wasn't the best coffee in town, but it was the strongest, hands down.

Just when I was considering pouting about the length of time it was taking her to get here, Lucy breezed through the door. Her blond hair was in a messy bun on top of her head, and she wore sweats and a wrinkled tee shirt. Lucy loved me enough to rush out the door without making herself beautiful. She waved at me and stepped up to order a drink.

I sighed. Telling Lucy my troubles would make me feel better, even if it didn't change anything.

She ordered a cinnamon latte and a vanilla bean scone and came over and sat across from me.

"So what's up?" she asked, setting her coffee and scone on the table and tucking her purse beneath it.

I leaned toward her. "Henry Hoffer was murdered last night," I whispered.

"What?" she exclaimed. Her eyes got big, and she froze.

"Shh! Keep your voice down," I hissed.

"How do you know?" she whispered.

I licked my thumb and reached across the table and rubbed it under her right eye. She really needed to remove her makeup before going to bed at night. She brushed my hand away and spit on a napkin and started cleaning up beneath her eyes.

"I found his body," I whispered, glancing around to make sure no one heard me.

She stopped mid rub, eyes wide again. "What? How?"

"I went by to see if he liked my pie, and there he was. Lying dead in a pool of blood, a steak knife in his chest."

"Oh no. That's horrible. What do the police say about it?"

I shook my head. "There was this detective there. I didn't know Sandy Harbor had a detective, did you?" She shook her head, and I continued. "I think they might suspect me."

"What? How could they suspect you?" she said too loudly.

I shushed her again. I looked around to see if anyone was listening, and I made eye contact with old Mr. Winters. He got up from his table across the room and shuffled toward us. Stopping at our table, he pulled out a chair and sat down and looked at me.

Lucy and I stared at him.

"You know, Henry and his employee, Charles Allen, argued the other day. I have never trusted Charles, myself. He has shifty eyes. I bet he did it," he said, his voice shaking with age.

Lucy and I glanced at each other again.

"How could you hear us from all the way over there?" I asked.

He pulled his hearing aid out of his ear. "This is the Sound Tone 5000. The most sensitive hearing aid on the market. I can hear most anything."

I nodded, mouth open. "Well, what did they argue about?"

"Money. Henry was tight with the money, and Charles hadn't had a raise in a couple of years. So I hear," he said and leaned back in his chair with a satisfied smile.

Who knew old Mr. Winters was a gossip? I glanced at Lucy. "We have to be going now. Thanks for the info," I told Mr. Winters and patted him on the shoulder as we left.

"Hey, that shoulda been worth a coffee, at least!" he called after us.

"I'll catch you next time," I called over my shoulder.

Out on the sidewalk, I leaned in close to Lucy. "Charles showed up not sixty seconds after I discovered Henry's body."

Lucy gasped. "Do you think he did it? Maybe he had just killed Henry, and then you showed up."

"That's a possibility," I said. How had Charles shown up like that, and I never heard his car? Only Henry's car had been in the parking lot. But Maybe Charles was parked on the next block so no one would recognize it.

"I bet that Charles Allen did it. Doesn't he strike you as a shady character?"

"Maybe. I don't know. But if there's a chance they'll blame me, I intend to investigate and find the real killer," I said.

"Okay. I'm with you," she said. "We'll find the killer."

Lucy was Ethel to my Lucy if that makes any sense. We were going to figure this out before I ended up in an orange prison jumpsuit. I don't look good in orange. It clashes with my red hair.

Chapter Six

IN THE MORNING I WENT for an extra-long run. I needed time to clear my head. The image of Henry lying dead on the floor of his restaurant kitchen was etched in my mind. I blamed Lucy. If she hadn't talked me into trying to go into the pie baking business, I never would have been there to find his body. I would have been just like everyone else in town, sitting in the local coffee shops, gossiping about it.

Sweat dribbled down my forehead as I drove home. I brushed it away and took a swig from my water bottle. When I pulled up to my house, my daughter Jennifer was sitting on the front steps. I still hadn't told her about what had happened. She was a worrier, that one.

I pulled into the driveway and got out of my car. "Hi, honey, what brings you by the old homestead so early in the morning?"

She shrugged. "I had nothing else to do."

That meant she missed me. College was only forty-five minutes away, but it was her first year away from home. She wanted to experience dorm life, but she also missed her mama. Jennifer was a homebody, and I knew college would be rough on her. She stood up, and I pulled her close for a hug. "I missed you!"

"Oh, Mom, you stink!" she said, wrinkling up her lightly freckled nose.

"It's called sweat. You know, from exercise?" I let her go and put my key in the door. "Why didn't you let yourself in?"

"I forgot my key," she said, following me into the house.

"And why was it off your keyring, young lady?" I said stripping off my windbreaker.

"I dunno. What are you making me for breakfast?" she asked, making a beeline to the kitchen and helping herself to the already brewed coffee.

"Cornflakes," I said, following her into the kitchen. I reached out a hand to rumple her strawberry blond hair. She took after me while my son Thad looked almost identical to his father; blond hair, blue eyes, and every bit as handsome. "Listen, Jennifer, there's something I need to tell you."

"I don't like the sound of that," she said. "What is it?"

There was a knock at the front door, and we both looked in that direction. "Wonder who that could be?" I said and went to answer it.

When I opened the door, Detective Blanchard stood on my doorstep. We stared at each other for a few seconds.

"Detective?" I said when I found my voice. Then I realized I was standing here in front of him, both stinky and sweaty, with my hair flying out from its ponytail, and no makeup. Yikes. A Southern woman has standards, and this wasn't it.

"Ms. McSwain, good morning. Please excuse my early appearance, but I wondered if I could have a few moments of your time?"

He stood there in his perfectly creased suit smelling of a fresh shower and rugged aftershave, and I wanted to tell him no. I needed a shower first. And even after that, I had no desire to talk about Henry Hoffer's murder. Ever.

"Uh," was all I could manage.

"It will only take a few moments," he reassured me. He held his notebook in one hand and a cell phone in the other.

Sighing, I nodded and opened the door for him to enter. I really didn't want to. Besides me being smelly, this man might want to hang a murder on me, and I kind of held it against him.

Jennifer turned around when she heard him enter, cup halfway to her lips and wide-eyed.

"Detective Blanchard, this is my daughter, Jennifer," I said.

He held his hand out and strode across the distance between them. Jennifer shook his hand, eyes still wide.

"Do you live here with your mother?" he asked her.

She narrowed her eyes at him. "Why do you want to know?"

That's my girl. She was just like her mother.

"Jennifer, that's what I was just getting ready to tell you. Henry Hoffer was murdered," I informed her. I didn't want my daughter to do something regretful, like tell the detective off. She wouldn't look good in an orange jumpsuit, either.

"What?" she asked, looking at me. "The old guy from the restaurant that carried disinfectant wipes everywhere he went? What happened?"

"He was murdered," the detective said. His eyes were on her, waiting for her reaction.

She looked at him. "And?"

"And I have a few questions for your mother."

Jennifer's head spun in my direction so fast, you'd have thought she was Linda Blair. "What did you do?"

"I didn't do anything!" I said and tilted my head toward the detective. *Way to take up for your mother.* "I was the first one to discover Henry's body. I had taken him a pie the night before, and I stopped by to see how he liked it."

Jennifer looked at me, puzzled. There were plenty of questions she wanted to ask, but thankfully, she held them for now.

"Would you like some coffee?" I asked the detective. My mother would kill me if I didn't show him hospitality, even if he was trying to lock me up for something I didn't do. Did Maine have a death penalty? I made a mental note to Google it.

"No, thank you. As I said, I only need a few moments of your time," he said. He stood there, looking slightly uncomfortable.

I relaxed a little. Maybe I could get rid of him fast. "So, Detective, what did you need to know?" I asked. "We can sit at the dining room table if you'd like."

"That would be great," he said and followed me to the dining room. "I was wondering, how well did you know Mr. Hoffer?"

"Well, like I said before, it's a small town. I certainly ran into him from time to time. And I ate at his restaurant probably once or twice a month," I said, taking a seat and offering him the one across from me.

He sat down and began writing in his notebook. "And did you ever see him socially?"

"What? Socially? No. Never." That was a weird question. Why would he ask that?

"And do you know his wife, Cynthia?" he asked, looking into my eyes now.

"I didn't even know he was married until Charles told me yesterday morning," I said, trying to sound convincing even though it was the truth. This man made me feel guilty, and I didn't know why.

"I see," he murmured and made another note.

"I didn't know Sandy Harbor had a detective," I said, changing the subject. He had ignored me the first time I brought it up, and it interested me.

He looked up at me. "I'm on loan from Bangor. It's a temporary thing."

"I see," I said. He had shown up at the restaurant with the other police, so he wasn't here specifically for Henry's murder. I wondered why the police had felt the need to borrow him from Bangor. Did we have that many murders in Sandy Harbor? If we did, I was completely ignorant of it.

He asked several more questions that seemed inconsequential, and the fact that they seemed inconsequential made me think there was some deep, dark motive he had for asking them. Like he was trying to trip me up. That's what detectives did, right?

"So, do you have any leads on the suspect?" I asked when it looked like he was getting ready to finish up. I couldn't help myself. I had to know if he really considered me a suspect.

"No, we're just doing a preliminary investigation right now," he said pleasantly.

"Do you think it might have been a botched robbery?" I asked. "I can't imagine anyone local murdering Henry. Maybe they jumped off of I-95 and thought they found an easy target for robbery, but things went bad, and Henry ended up dead."

"Robbery? No. We didn't find any evidence of a robbery."

That was disappointing. "Well, I happened to hear that Charles Allen argued with Henry recently." It was out of my mouth before I could stop it. I wanted to slap my hand across my mouth. That was gossip, and I shouldn't have said it.

His eyebrows shot up. "Really? And do you happen to know what that argument was about?"

"Money. I heard Henry hadn't given Charles a raise in a couple of years." In for a penny, in for a pound. I may as well tell him what I knew.

"I see," he said and made a note. "Henry's widow said Henry thought highly of Charles. I would think if Henry liked him, he would have made sure he was well compensated, but you never know in situations like this. I appreciate your help, Ms. McSwain. Can you think of anything else that might be helpful?"

I felt guilty about throwing Charles under the bus. Shutting my mouth was probably the smartest move I could make. I shook my head. "No, sorry."

He nodded. "Well then, I've got to be going. Thanks again for your time, Ms. McSwain." He got to his feet.

"Missus," I corrected him.

He looked at me quizzically.

"I'm a missus, even if my husband is gone," I said, and then I immediately felt foolish for bringing it up.

"Oh, I do apologize. I didn't mean anything by it," he said, tilting his head to look at me.

"No problem," I said. I could feel my cheeks turn pink, and I silently cursed myself for saying anything.

"Well, I'll get out of your hair," he said and nodded.

I showed him to the door and hoped I wouldn't have to see him again. Maybe he'd figure out who the killer was, and this thing would be over and done with today. Fat chance.

Lucy was standing on my doorstep when I swung the door open, and when she saw the detective, her eyes got big. I quickly introduced them, and he made his exit without making conversation with her. He wasn't much of a talker, that one.

We stood on the step and watched the detective get in his car and drive off.

"Wow. He's quite a looker," Lucy said, still looking down the street after him.

"Quite a looker that wants to put me in an orange jumpsuit," I reminded her and went back into the house.

Lucy followed me inside. "Hey, Jennifer!" she said when she saw my daughter.

"Hey, Lucy. What's up with my mom being a suspect in a murder?" Jennifer asked her. "What goes on around here when I'm not here?"

Lucy shrugged her shoulders. "I don't know, but we are going to have to find the real murderer and clear your mom's name. Otherwise, We'll have to spend our weekends visiting her at the county lockup from here on out."

"I'm not going to the county lockup every weekend. I've got studies."

"Thanks, Jennifer." I rolled my eyes and got two cups from the cupboard and handed one to Lucy. "I don't like that he seems to suspect me. He told me Henry thought highly of Charles," I said. They both looked at me.

"What?" Lucy said. "But old man Winters said he argued with Henry over money."

"I know. But if Henry's wife is vouching for Charles, who is going to vouch for me? I think we have some work to do," I said. "Maybe Henry liked Charles, but not enough to give him a raise. And maybe that made Charles angry enough to kill Henry."

"Money makes people do crazy things," Lucy agreed. "Some people kill over a few bucks."

I filled both of our cups with coffee and turned to her. "Right? And you know Henry was so cheap he only paid Charles a few bucks. That would make anyone kill."

"What if his wife did it?" Jennifer asked and took a sip of her coffee. "Lots of wives kill their husbands."

"That's true, too," I agreed. "We need answers. We need to dig up the dirt on Charles or his wife so that detective will leave me alone."

"Let's come up with a plan." Lucy went to the refrigerator and pulled out the bottle of French vanilla creamer, and we took a seat at the kitchen table.

Figuring out who killed Henry was going to be hard, but I hoped it wouldn't be as hard as doing time for murder.

Chapter Seven

I whipped up some pancakes, and we gathered around the kitchen table and dug in. I had bought more than ten pounds of apples, so I chopped some up and added apple pie spice to them and folded them into the pancake batter. I was thinking today's pie would be a Dutch crust apple pie. One of my favorites.

"So Allie, I have a question for you," Lucy said and took a bite of her pancake.

"Shoot," I said and immediately regretted it. Maybe I should remove all words that sounded murderous from my vocabulary.

Lucy looked at me pointedly, and I knew she had read my mind. She was scary that way sometimes. I shrugged.

"Did you do it?"

I looked at her. "Do what?"

"Murder Henry."

I narrowed my eyes at her. "How on earth can you ask such a thing? I would never kill Henry or anyone else for that matter! The nerve!"

"Okay, okay. I know you didn't do it, but I had to ask. Just like in the movies, they always ask the suspect if they did it, even if they're not a very likely suspect," she said and got up to pour another cup of coffee. She was wearing a short yellow miniskirt.

It was completely wrong for the approaching fall weather, but Lucy liked her short skirts.

"Well, I can't imagine anyone thinking that I did it," I said, still feeling more than a little miffed. "I can't stand the sight of blood."

"You do have a temper, Mom," Jennifer pointed out. "Maybe Henry was rude like he usually was, and then you lost it and killed him."

I narrowed my eyes at her. "Maybe if I had kids that had listened to me when they were little, my temper never would have developed," I said.

"All right, all right," Lucy said, sitting back down at the table. "We need to think about how to figure out who the killer is. You say you discovered the body, and then Charles showed up right away?"

"Yes. Like less than a minute later, I'd say." I took a swig of my now cold coffee. Even tepid coffee was tasty.

"Any chance he was hiding there in the restaurant?" she asked and poured more syrup on her pancakes.

"I don't think so. I entered through the back door, and then he came in behind me."

"He could have been there earlier and committed the crime," Jennifer said, "and then slipped out the front door and waited for someone else to discover the body."

"Yeah, they say the murderer always returns to the scene of the crime," Lucy pointed out. "I think Jennifer has a good point."

"The movies and television shows say that, but has that ever happened in real life? It would be dumb because if you're the murderer, you're right there under the cops' noses. They would question you, and you might give yourself away. It doesn't make sense," I said, and in my mind, I went over the details of what had happened. After thinking about it, I said, "but you know, Charles has a key to the front door. Jennifer could be right. He could have gone out the front and then re-entered through the back. But even so, I don't know why he would."

"Was the body still warm?" Jennifer asked. "Was it gross?"

"I don't know, I wasn't going to touch him. When the police got there, he was already gone and probably had been for a while."

Lucy shook her head. "Poor Henry."

"I think they need to question people that weren't there. Obviously, I couldn't have murdered Henry since Charles showed up right away. I wouldn't have had time," I pointed out.

"But you didn't touch the body to see if it was warm? You could have done it hours earlier, and he would have already been cold when the cops got there. I bet that's what the police are thinking," Jennifer pointed out, running a finger through the syrup on her plate and sticking it in her mouth.

I was beginning to wonder if this was my kid. What happened to protecting your family?

"We need to interrogate Charles," Lucy said. "That should be our first order of business."

"Interrogate is a strong word. We need to keep our police jargon under control," I said, pushing my plate back. I was losing my appetite.

"So let's do it. Let's go find him and let's find out what he knows," Lucy said.

I picked up my now empty plate and took it to the sink and rinsed the remaining syrup off of it. Would Charles even talk to us? He must know he's as much a suspect as I was.

"Yes?" Lucy tossed at me when I didn't answer.

"I guess," I said. "I mean, I don't know that he would tell us anything useful. Why would he if he is the murderer?"

"He might slip up," Jennifer pointed out. "We can talk to him. It won't hurt anything."

I sighed. "I guess so."

I didn't have a good feeling about this. I needed to clear my name, but I also didn't want to mess with someone that might have committed murder. If Charles had done it, then he had one kill under his belt, and what was to stop him from making it two?

"I know, you can bake him a pie, and we'll take it over to him," Lucy said. "Say it's to comfort him because of the stress and trauma of yesterday."

"That's a great idea," Jennifer said, nodding.

I looked from one to the other. What was I getting myself into? This had to be folly. I sighed. "Okay. But if we end up in orange jumpsuits, you are both going to pay."

I hoped Charles liked apple pie because that was what he was going to get.

Chapter Eight

I had baked the pie and let it cool enough to handle, and then we were on our way. Jennifer opted out of the trip. Lot of support I got from her. We found Charles's address on the Internet and didn't even have to pay for it. Lucy drove while I held the pie, and when we got to his house, I was more than a little surprised. Charles had a pretty nice house for a fry cook. It was a two-story Craftsman style. It looked to be more than a couple thousand square feet.

I looked over at Lucy. Her eyebrows lifted in an "oh my goodness, will you look at that" look, but she didn't say a word.

We got out and went to the door. I rang the bell, and we waited. Charles had yellow and white daisies in a planter on the porch. There was the sound of movement coming from inside, and the door swung open. When he got a look at who was standing on his porch, his mouth dropped open in surprise.

"What do you want?"

"Why, Charles, I'm just being neighborly. I brought you a Dutch crust apple pie," I purred.

"I don't remember you being my neighbor," he said, not taking his eyes off the pie I held. I hadn't bothered using a pie keeper after what happened to the last one. Dead Henry or not, I couldn't replace another one of grandmama's pie keepers.

"Hello, Charles," Lucy said brightly.

"May we come in?" I asked sweetly.

He looked at me and then down at the pie. "Yeah, sure. I guess so."

We followed him into the kitchen. His house was surprisingly modern looking. I say surprisingly because he seemed a little redneck. There was just something about him.

"What a lovely home you have," I said and made a beeline for the kitchen, setting the pie down on the kitchen table.

"Thanks. What kind of pie did you say that was?" He was leering at the pie now.

"Dutch crust apple pie. Get me some plates, and we'll have a piece," I said. I looked at Lucy, smiling at her. Food really was the way to a man's heart. Or, hopefully, to the information he knew about the murder. Or a confession. Whichever.

He got out plates, forks, and a knife, and I served us.

"This is terrific," he said around a mouthful of pie. He wasn't holding back on the pie. Charles was no delicate flower when it came to food.

"Thank you, Charles. I, uh, I was just wondering. Who do you think might have murdered Henry?" I thought I would ask the obvious question first.

He shrugged. "I don't know. Henry was the cantankerous sort. Could have been anyone."

I narrowed my eyes at him. That wasn't much help. "Yes, but you would think that if someone went to the trouble of killing him, they would have to have a reason. A really good one. No one just goes and murders someone without a good reason."

"I dunno. There's no telling. There are crazy people in this world," he said and finished up the rest of his piece of pie.

"Here, help yourself to another piece," I said, pushing the pie toward him.

"Why'd you bring this over here?" he asked. Suspicion was setting in, but it didn't stop him from cutting a wedge twice the size of the first. "I been living in this house for six years and in this town my whole life, and you never brought me a pie."

"I thought it would be nice. What with that horrible trauma we both experienced when we found Henry. I thought this would make us both feel better," I said, glancing at Lucy. She sat entranced, watching Charles shovel the slab of pie into his mouth.

"It's great," he said, and when he opened his mouth, a piece of crust fell out. I winced.

"Thanks," I said, looking away. "But surely there has to be someone that Henry had a problem with, say, in the past couple of weeks? Maybe someone owed him money? Or was there someone he argued with?" There. A little bait might help.

He shrugged his shoulders. "Nope. Not that I can think of."

I breathed air out through my mouth. Darn him.

Lucy was staring at him. "How about you?"

I nearly gave myself whiplash when my head whipped around to look at her. I raised my eyebrows at her.

"What about me?" he asked, looking at her, fork poised in the air.

"Did you do it? Did you murder Henry Hoffer?" She narrowed her eyes at him, and I wanted to snatch that blonde curly hair right off her head.

"What? What are you talking about?" he asked, staring at her with his fork still midway to his mouth.

"We heard you argued with Henry a week ago," she said, leaning toward him.

"Um, what Lucy means is, well, is there any chance you might have argued with Henry?" I asked. What on earth was she thinking?

He narrowed his eyes at Lucy. "No. No, I did not murder Henry."

"Oh, that's good," I said. "We were so worried someone might blame you." We were playing good cop, bad cop now.

Then he turned on me. "You were there first. Did you murder him? I heard you arguing with him in his office the night before."

"Me? What? No!" I exclaimed. "I could never murder anyone! And we weren't arguing. We were discussing pie."

"Yeah? Well, if we're throwing out accusations, then I guess I have a right to throw one of my own out there. And if that detective comes by here, I just might throw it to him."

"Don't you threaten her," Lucy said. "We know you had money problems and that Henry wouldn't give you a raise."

I clamped my hand over her mouth. We didn't need Charles knowing everything that we knew.

"What she means is, there's a rumor on the street." I smiled sweetly.

Charles stared at us, mouth open.

I gave Lucy the eye, and she squirmed out from behind my hand.

She straightened her hair. "So, where were you on the night of the murder?" she continued, much calmer.

"I was visiting my mom," he said and licked pie off his thumb. "You two have a lot of nerve coming over here and accusing me of murdering my boss."

"Your mom?" I asked, ignoring that last part.

"At the nursing home," he said. "And now, if you ladies would please take a hike, I would appreciate it. But leave the rest of the pie."

I stared at him. "Your mother is in a nursing home?"

"That's what I said."

I stood up. He had an alibi. There would be nurses, aides, and residents at a nursing home. Several of which had to have seen him.

"Oh, and if you're so hot to catch a killer, maybe you should have taken note that the gardener was there the night before," he said, leaning back in his chair.

"So? What of it?" I asked.

"Henry argued with him over the new flowers he was supposed to put in the planters out front. Henry wanted all yellow and the gardener, Ralph Henderson, brought orange and yellow."

I gasped. He was right. The gardener had been planting flowers the night before. And not only that, some of his tools were still in the planter the next morning. What gardener leaves his tools laying out overnight in a planter? Some hooligan could easily make off with them. It was as if he had taken off in a hurry. Or maybe he had stopped to murder Henry and then left in a hurry before the police showed up. Why hadn't I thought of this earlier?

"Uh-huh. I got smarts too, you know," he said, tapping his forehead.

"Yes. So I see. Come on, Lucy."

We made our exit.

When we got into the car, my phone rang. It was my son, Thad.

"Hi honey," I said when I answered it.

"Mom, Jennifer said you were suspected of murder. Did you kill someone?" he asked, his voice squeaking on the word 'kill'.

"Way to have faith in your mom, Thad. Of course I didn't kill anyone," I insisted. "Do you really think I would do something like that?"

"No, I didn't think so," he said with a sigh. "But if you had, I want you to know it wouldn't change our relationship in the least. I'd go down to the prison and put money on your books every month. That way you could buy yourself a candy bar and live it up."

"That's comforting," I said and sighed. "When are you coming home for a visit?"

Thad was at the University of Wisconsin at Madison. His visits were getting fewer and fewer, it seemed. I missed my first-born.

"Mom, school just started a few weeks ago. I just spent the whole summer with you," he said, sounding annoyed.

"Summer was a long time ago."

He chuckled. "I just wanted you to know that if you need someone to take Dixie while you're in the slammer, it will have to be Grandma."

"You're so thoughtful. Grandma is allergic," I said.

"I gotta go, Mom. I'm glad you didn't kill anyone. Let me know how things are going," he said. "Love you."

"Love you too—," I was interrupted by dead airspace. He had hung up. I glanced over at Lucy sitting next to me and rolled my eyes.

"He's such a good boy," she said with a grin.

"That, he is." Both my kids were good kids. I wasn't sure where they got their smart-aleck personalities.

Chapter Nine

"So what do you think? Was he telling the truth?" Lucy asked, her hands curled around a cup of joe.

I shrugged. "He seemed sincere. And he was visiting his mother."

"He was sincere about your pie, is what he was sincere about," she said, raising the cup to her lips. "We need to visit his mother. How do we know he was really visiting her?"

"Lucy, she's in a nursing home. There would have been a lot of people there to vouch for him."

She shrugged. "We should still talk to her."

I placed a ball of pie dough on the flour-covered dishtowel and began to roll it out. My grandmama always taught me to lay out a flour-sack dishtowel on the counter and sprinkle it with flour before rolling the pie crust. Fortunately, I had a stack of her old flour-sack dishtowels, because those were hard to come by these days. The kind the stores tried to pass off as authentic weren't quite the same.

"I don't think it matters much. I mean, what mama is going to rat out her son and say he wasn't there?" I said, turning the dishtowel so I could get at the other side of the piecrust.

"True. But I think we need to investigate," she said. "What kind of pie are you making today?"

"Sour cream apple. I think I'm going to take it over to Martha Newberry, poor thing."

"What? I love sour cream apple. Can't you just take her a piece of it?"

I gave her a look. "You should have seen her. She was just beside herself. I'm sure she's never seen such an awful thing as when Henry was lying dead on the floor. I certainly hadn't."

"Say, how are you holding up after that? No nightmares? Or weird thoughts?" she asked, getting up to pour herself another cup of coffee.

"No nightmares. Although sometimes the image of Henry's body laying on the floor skates across my mind." I shuddered. I didn't want to admit it, but it was happening a lot. I figured it would stop at some point. Surely it would after some time had passed.

She came over to me and hugged me. "I've got to get to work. If you need me for anything, let me know."

"Thanks, Lucy."

Lucy worked in a flower shop part-time. Her husband was an accountant and did quite well, but Lucy enjoyed getting out and being able to talk to people. Sometimes I thought I needed to take a part-time job just to get out of the house, but then I realized I would be at someone else's beck and call, and I liked my freedom.

I KNOCKED ON MARTHA Newberry's door and waited. A dog yipped from inside, and I hoped I wasn't interrupting her afternoon nap. When she didn't come to the door, I knocked again. I carried the pie in a reusable shopping bag. It was brand new and cute, with singing apple pies all over the front. It advertised Shaw's Market.

After a bit, I heard footsteps, and I could tell she was peeking through the peephole on her door. I smiled real big, and the door swung slowly open.

"Yes?" she said, peering around the door. A little tan Chihuahua peered from behind her and barked at me.

"Good afternoon Martha, how are you? I thought I'd bring you a pie," I said cheerfully. She looked tired, with dark circles under her eyes. Poor thing.

She brightened when I held up the bag. "A pie? How sweet of you, Allie. Come on in. Now, Tiny, you hush." She opened the door wider, and I followed her in. Tiny took a few steps back, unsure whether he should allow me to enter.

Martha shuffled along; her body bent slightly and led me to her living room. "Have a seat," she said. She took the pie from me and set it on the pass-through window to her kitchen.

"You have a lovely home," I said, sitting down on the cabbage rose print sofa. The entire room was done in pink. Pink carpets, drapes, and throw pillows. It felt like 1984 in here. I smiled. My grandmama would have loved it.

Tiny sat across from me and kept an eye on me, but had stopped his barking.

"Thank you, dear," she said. "Can I get you some tea?"

"No, thank you," I said. Northerners' idea of tea was hot, with milk and sugar, while mine was cold and sweet. "I wanted to check on you after that terrible fright we had the other day."

"Oh dear, that really was terrible," she said, sitting across from me on the matching love seat. "My, my, my. I have never seen such a thing. I've been having trouble sleeping ever since." She had a far-off look in her eyes, and I knew she was remembering that horrible scene.

"Me either," I murmured. It truly was horrible. I got up and sat beside her and took her hand and patted it. "I'm sorry you had to see that."

She looked me in the eye. "Who would do such an unimaginable thing? Why, I've lived here all my life, and we've had so little violence around here. Oh, there was that time that Ritter woman killed her husband in a fit of jealous rage, and once a man killed his wife and then killed himself. I can't remember who that was now. But to just have a random murder like that? I just don't know what this world is coming to."

"I know, it's very shocking. The police are getting help from that detective they borrowed from Bangor though, so I'm sure they'll figure it out."

She got lost in her thoughts for a few moments, and I looked over at the La-Z-Boy at the end of the living room. There was a pair of men's slippers next to it and a pipe on the end table. A pair of men's gold-rimmed reading glasses and a folded up newspaper was also on the table. A walker stood on the other side of the chair. Mr. Newberry had died several years earlier.

Martha caught me looking at the chair. She smiled. "I haven't had the heart to put his things away," she said softly. "We went out to dinner that night at Henry's, and George expected to come home afterward and smoke his pipe and read his paper. Just like any other evening."

My heart broke. I knew exactly how she felt. It was still difficult for me to think about Thaddeus without breaking down and crying. "I understand. I lost my husband a few years ago, too. It's the hardest thing I've ever been through. That's the reason I started my blog. To help others and myself who are going through this. Grief is a terrible thing."

She looked at me, puzzled. "Blog? Is that one of those computer type things?"

"Yes, it's sort of an online journal," I explained. Poor Martha. Just like Henry, she hadn't come into the computer age, and probably never would.

"I see," she said absently. "I have been feeling so tired lately."

"I'm sorry. I know this whole thing has had me exhausted, too. I shouldn't keep you," I said and stood up. "Martha, is there anything else I can get you or do for you? I'd be happy to help."

"No, dear, I'm fine. But, I suppose, if you wouldn't mind, perhaps someday you'd come by, and we can talk about our husbands? You know, just to keep one another company?"

I had to choke back the lump forming in my throat. "Of course, Martha. I would love to do that." How had I not thought to check in on her before? I knew her husband had died several years ago, and other than attending the funeral, I hadn't offered her a bit of support. I felt terrible about that. "It must have been hard, working at Henry's after your husband died there."

"It was, but Henry was so good to me. I don't know what I would have done without him," she said, smiling sweetly.

"It's good to have friends help you through hard times," I said.

She carefully got to her feet, and I offered her a steadying hand. "I do appreciate the pie so much. I don't bake anymore now that it's just me and Tiny," she said and shuffled her way with me to the door.

"I'm happy to bring it to you. It doesn't freeze as well as some of my pies, but it will keep a few days in the refrigerator," I said. "I bake frequently, so I'll drop back by and bring you something else, and we can have that talk. Oh, let me give you one of my business cards. You can call me whenever you'd like." I dug through my purse and found one of the business cards I used for my blog and gave it to her, then hugged her on my way out the door.

I really needed to form some sort of support group locally. Lots of the elderly were without their spouses and loved ones, and it had to be lonely for them. I made a mental note to come up with a plan to help with that.

Chapter Ten

The sun was rising later in the mornings these days and I decided I needed to allow myself to sleep in thirty minutes later the next day. The running trail was lit, but I wasn't comfortable running in the dark anymore. You never knew if the crazies were hiding behind the bushes along the trail. I'm talking about the regular town crazies. And now there was also a murderer on the loose.

My feet echoed in the silent early morning air as they hit the paved trail. I was four miles into a ten-mile run. I had hit my sweet spot and wasn't feeling any pain. I breathed in and out in rhythm with my footsteps. I wondered if I could really run 26.2 miles. Ten was the farthest I had ever run, and that last mile and a half were rough. I needed to research how other runners got themselves through the hard parts.

I was listening to Boston on my iPod, leaving one earbud out so I could hear if anyone slipped up behind me. Classic rock was the best for running. The dangling earbud slapped against my side, and I noticed a car parked at the corner up ahead. The path crossed several streets, and someone was leaning against a dark SUV parked on Church Street. My heart jumped a little, and I debated on turning off the path to avoid whoever it was.

The sun was in my eyes, and I was having a hard time seeing them. I slowed down, keeping an eye on the person.

I realized it was Detective Blanchard when I had run a few more steps. What was he doing out here this early? He stood up straighter as I got closer to him.

"Hello, Allie," he called.

"Hey," I said, breathing hard. I came to a stop in front of him. "Well, did you come out for a run?" I looked him up and down in his suit. He really needed to loosen up.

He cracked a slight smile. "I'll hit the gym later this evening. I wanted to speak to you for a minute."

I gave him a level gaze. "It was important enough to hang around the running trail this early in the morning? You couldn't call me?"

"No, actually I was headed to the station and remembered that you run in the early mornings, so I thought I'd stop and see if you were around. And here you are," he said, motioning toward me.

"Here I am," I said and forced myself to smile. I waited. There wasn't any reason for him to search me out this early in the morning, regardless of the reason he gave.

He looked uncomfortable for a moment and then continued. "I heard that you and Henry Hoffer argued the night before the murder. Care to tell me about that?"

Charles! He had squealed on me after I made him a pie. Now I was angry. I put my hands on my hips. "I told you. I wanted him to try my pie while it was still warm. Apple pie needs to be warm when you eat it."

"So you argued about it? It's that important?" he asked. He had somehow whipped out his notebook without me seeing it. He began jotting down notes.

"No, it isn't that important, but I was hoping Henry, and I could do business together. Eating it warm was important in this instance. It would have been important to my new business." I felt like an idiot. I had argued with someone about eating pie while it was warm. What was I thinking?

"I see," he said and made another note.

"I don't think you do see. Charles told you we argued, didn't he?" I asked, trying to keep my voice calm. Charles and I were going to have to have another talk.

"I'm not really at liberty to say," he said, looking at me again.

"I cannot believe you are asking me about this, right here on the running path this early in the morning," I said. I was losing the fight with my temper. "I mean, really? Really? I had no quarrel with Henry, and it wasn't a real argument, anyway. These Northerners, no, *you* Northerners, can be difficult and cantankerous and I was simply making sure he understood that it was important to the taste and texture of the pie. It meant nothing at all." My Southern accent was coming out thicker than it had in a long time. Pretty soon I would be saying 'y'all,' and 'hush my mouth.' My temper did that to me.

He blinked at me. "I'm sorry, Mrs. McSwain. I don't mean to upset you, but I am investigating a murder. A murder, I might point out, that you discovered. I have to investigate all leads, and my current lead is you." His eyes had narrowed, and I thought he might have a little temper of his own. I bet a lot of police officers did. They dealt with terrible situations and bad people.

Why wouldn't they get upset about the things they saw every day?

I took a deep breath. I needed to calm down before I found myself in handcuffs. "Okay, then. It wasn't really an argument. I had nothing against Henry. Do you have any other questions?"

He looked at me silently for a few moments. "You don't have an alibi, Mrs. McSwain, do you?"

My mouth dropped open. Was that a threat?

"Of course I do. I was at home. Watching television." Alone. Without an alibi.

He leaned back against his vehicle and studied me.

When he didn't say anything for a few moments, I couldn't keep quiet. "Well, are there fingerprints on the knife? Did you even think to look?" I knew I was pushing things. I should have kept my mouth shut, but I was beyond irritated.

He chuckled dryly. "There were no fingerprints. The knife was either wiped clean, or the killer wore gloves. Why do you ask?"

All right, I had gone too far. I needed to reel this thing in. "Look, Detective Blanchard. I apologize if I sound defensive. It's just that I've never been suspected in a murder before, and I'm a little out of sorts. I don't know who killed Henry, and if I did, I would tell you."

He stood up and pulled his car keys out of his pocket. "I'll be in touch, Mrs. McSwain." He got in the car and slammed the door without so much as a 'see ya later.'

I watched him drive off, and it took everything I had to keep from breaking down and crying. What had I gotten myself into? I should have kept my mouth shut. Now he was even more suspicious of me than ever.

I turned around and headed back down the trail toward my car. Forget the run. My heart wasn't in it anymore.

Chapter Eleven

I t was Tuesday before I saw Lucy again. She did that sometimes; disappearing for a few days. She had work. She had her husband. Who could blame her? I had been knee-deep in a blog article anyway, so I hardly missed her. Sort of. It had been ten days since Henry's murder. What was taking them so long to figure out who did it?

I kept expecting the detective to stop by my house or meet me again on the running trail, but he had made himself scarce. I wondered why he wasn't asking me more questions and following me around town, trying to find a motive. But... nothing. And that nothing just made me more paranoid. Had he put a tail on me? That was police lingo. I was watching reruns of Hill Street Blues and picking it up. Maybe the police were so good at tailing suspects that they blended in, and you never saw them.

I heard the front door open, and Lucy called out. At the sound of her voice, I felt like a blue tick hound about to go out on its first hunt of the season. Lucy was here!

"In here," I called, restraining myself from jumping into her arms.

"Are you ready to go?" Lucy asked me, coming to lean over my shoulder and reading what I had just written. We were going to see if we could find out anything from the gardener, Ralph Henderson.

"Do you mind not reading over my shoulder?" I asked and hit save.

Grief is a funny thing. Just when you think you have things under control, it pops up again. That was the subject of my blog post. With the anniversary of Thaddeus's death approaching, it seemed like a natural topic.

"You're putting it up on a blog for the whole world to read. What difference does it make?" She took a step back, and I got to my feet and gave her a quick hug.

"It's just the idea of having someone reading over my shoulder is all," I said, trying not to sound grumpy.

"Do you think writing about grief is making you continue to grieve?" she suddenly asked.

I looked at her. She may have had a point, but I had been doing this for so long, it was part of who I was. "No," I answered. "I'm fine. I'm doing a good thing. It helps others with their grief."

"I wasn't saying you weren't. Honestly, Allie, you are one of the most compassionate women I know. I just worry about you sometimes." She looked away when she said it. She knew she was treading on thin ice. I needed this blog. I really did. Just like I needed the pies. Both were therapy.

I forced myself to smile and decided to ignore the comment. "Let's go," I said. We headed to the front door, and I grabbed my purse on the way out. Sometimes I wondered if I grieved more than I should. At this point, shouldn't I have been past falling apart at Thaddeus's memory? When one of my readers asked this question, I always assured them that grief was subjective and couldn't be rushed. Everyone's normal was different. But if I had to be honest, I had to admit that now and then, I wondered if what I was going through was normal. If I was normal. I sighed.

We took my car. We had no idea where Ralph Henderson lived, but it didn't matter. He was one of only three professional gardeners in town so we would find him working in someone's yard or some business' planters.

"I'm sorry," Lucy said without looking at me.

"It's okay," I said, pulling into the Cup and Bean's drive-thru. The smell of coffee brewing filled the crisp fall air. I placed our order and pulled up to the window.

"Oh look, is that him?" Lucy said, peering over her sunglasses and pointing.

I squinted at the figure bending over a planter in front of the dentist's office across the street. "I think so," I said. We got our drinks, and I gunned it out of there. I hit the green light just right and was across the street in a jiffy.

"Hey, Baretta, slow down some," Lucy said, gripping the armrest on the passenger side door.

"Yeah, yeah," I answered. Everyone's a critic.

I pulled into a nearby parking space, and we both got out.

"Hey, Ralph," I said, turning on the Southern charm as we approached. "How y'all doing today?"

He looked up at me and then went right back to planting orange marigolds. I wondered if the dentist had wanted yellow. If so, he had better not complain about it. It might be the death of him.

"Uh, Ralph, we'd like to talk to you a second if you don't mind," I said, trying again.

He ignored me. But Lucy was not to be put off.

"Hey, Ralph, we're talking to you."

He glanced in her direction, then settled a plant into the hole he had dug for it. "I don't have time for talkin'. I got work to do."

"Well, we want to know where you were the night of Henry Hoffer's murder," she said, sounding tough. I glanced at her. She had the swagger down pat. I needed to work on that.

He sniffed and then stabbed the ground with his garden spade. Suddenly a picture of him stabbing a steak knife into Henry's chest flashed in front of my eyes. "I don't see that that's any of your business, now is it?"

If I didn't know better, I would swear that Ralph had suddenly taken on a New Jersey accent. A New Jersey mobster's accent.

"Now, Ralph, what Lucy means is, we are just trying to help Henry's widow out as much as possible. The poor thing is fraught with worry as to who could have done such a horrible thing," I said. "We just wondered if you saw anyone suspicious hanging around. And I had noticed your tools in the planter in front of the restaurant."

There. That should do the trick. Never mind that we had yet to meet Henry's wife.

He slowly turned his head in my direction and looked me over. Uh oh. The last thing I wanted to do was make a possible murderer mad at me. I smiled real big, tilted my head, and twirled a lock of my red hair. I was harmless.

"Is that a threat?" he asked.

"Oh, goodness, no! We're just trying to help. Honest." My heart was pounding in my chest, but I just kept smiling.

He stared at me a minute longer and then sniffed. "I went fishing."

"Oh. Oh, I see," I said.

"And you were in such a hurry to go fishing that you left your tools out in the open where anyone could steal them?" Lucy said, leaning toward him. "I ain't buying it."

"Look, lady, whoever you are, I don't owe you any explanations. Get out of here. I have work to do." His neck was turning red, and I decided we would be better off some place else. Any place else. This guy was going to blow.

"Well, we'll just be going," I said and grabbed Lucy's arm.

"Well, I don't believe it," Lucy said, hands on hips. "It seems mighty suspicious if you ask me."

"Now, Lucy, let's not go making accusations," I pleaded.

Ralph took a couple of steps toward Lucy. This was going to turn out very badly.

"Now look, Ralph, I apologize for Lucy's behavior. We didn't mean to come here and cause trouble. It's just that the police are suspicious of town folk, and honestly, I can't think of one town person that would commit such a horrible crime. Is there anything else you can tell us? Did you see anything that evening when you were there? A suspicious car?" I tried to appeal to his sense of community and hoped he would help us out.

He threw his hands into the air. "I told you. I went fishing. I was out on the ocean most of the night and slept in the next day until nearly noon. Now get out of here." He turned back to his work, pulling the spade out of the ground.

"And you just forgot your tools in the planter?" I asked. I didn't want to push him, but I didn't understand why he would leave them behind.

"I was excited to go fishing," he said without looking at me.

Lucy snorted. "Right."

We weren't going to get anything out of him, so I managed to get Lucy back in the car before she got us murdered. I wondered if poor Henry had made an accusation against Ralph, and that was how he ended up with a steak knife in his chest.

I WORE MY PLAIN BLACK dress to the funeral. I hadn't worn it since Thaddeus's funeral, and I made a mental note to get rid of it. I could buy something new for any further funeral attendance. God forbid there should be any more for a while.

Lucy and I sat in the back, watching the mourners file in. Lucy wore a short hot pink skirt with a white top. She stood out like a sore thumb. Lucy was an attention grabber.

"We need to keep our eye out for anyone suspicious," she leaned over and whispered to me.

I nodded. It had now been eleven days since Henry had died, and rumor had it a relative coming from Spain had held things up. I had been watching everyone carefully, but there weren't any strangers that had shown up yet. I had known everyone here for years, or I at least knew who they were. Small towns were like that. If you didn't know them personally, they were still familiar faces you passed in the grocery store or saw at the movie theater on Saturday nights.

Henry's widow sat in the first row, dabbing her eyes with a hanky. She was older than I had expected, but it could have been the fact that her hair was a solid gray. I wondered where she and Henry had met. Charles had said she was from Chicago. Maybe she had argued with her husband and, in a fit of rage, killed him? She didn't seem the type. I don't know how I knew it, but I did. And as soon as I had that thought, I thought maybe that was exactly the type that would kill someone. I sighed. I was going to drive myself crazy over this thing.

I looked up as an older couple went to the widow, greeted her, and sat down beside her. I didn't know them, so I guessed they were the relatives from Spain.

"I like that dress," Lucy said, admiring the black dress with red flowers that the woman next to Henry's widow wore.

"It is very pretty," I agreed.

Charles and Ralph were both in attendance. Charles sat behind the grieving widow, a little close to the family pew if you ask me. I would have only expected family in the first several rows and very close friends after that. But this wasn't the South, so maybe Charles didn't know the protocol.

Ralph sat in what looked to be the exact middle of the room. I decided that by itself was suspicious.

I tried to listen to the sermon, but in my mind, I kept seeing poor dead Henry with a knife sticking out of him. I wondered what it was like to breathe your last breath. What were your last thoughts? Did you think about your loved ones? Your regrets? I shook myself. That kind of thinking would drive a person mad.

The first year after Thaddeus's death, I had imagined his last moments, over and over. I thought I would end up in a mental hospital.

At the close of the service, we got up and filed past the open casket. I cringed and followed Lucy. I had no desire to look at him, and I wished his widow had gone for a closed casket. Closed casket was always best.

I stared at Lucy's back as we slowly filed by, determined not to look. But at the last second, I did look, and for a moment, Henry opened his eyes and beckoned to me with his cold, dead finger. I slapped a hand over my mouth to keep from screaming. When I blinked, his eyes were closed again, and he looked like he was taking a nap.

At the cemetery, I introduced myself to Henry's widow, Cynthia Hoffer. She pasted on a smile, but her eyes were far away. I knew the look. I also knew the thoughts going through her mind. Losing a loved one was heartbreaking. She was genuinely grieving, and I knew she was not the killer. I gave her one of my business cards with my blog address on it and told her to call me if she needed someone to talk to.

Henry wanted me to find his killer. I was sure of that.

Chapter Twelve

"So we got nothin'," Lucy said, cutting a piece of raisin apple pie.

The spicy scent of the pie filled the kitchen. "Pretty much," I said, pouring two big glasses of milk.

She handed me a plate with a piece of pie on it and cut one for herself. "Back to the drawing board."

I didn't know whether to feel hopeful or disheartened since I hadn't heard anything from the detective. Maybe he had another suspect, and I was off the hook. Or maybe he was planning his strategy to put me in a nice pair of orange coveralls. I sighed.

"Cheer up, buttercup. We'll figure this out," Lucy said, taking a bite of pie. "Mmm, this is really good. New recipe?"

"Not really. I just made a few small changes. I used brown sugar instead of white and doubled the nutmeg," I answered. I loved experimenting with recipes. And I loved nutmeg. Adding extra nutmeg was always a win.

"It's wonderful," she said around the pie in her mouth.

"Maybe I should call Detective Blanchard? Maybe he's moved on from suspecting me, and he'll tell me so, and I can just forget the whole thing," I said. Talk about wishful thinking.

"No, if you're still a suspect, then you'll look like you're desperate and trying to get information," Lucy said. "No use drawing attention to yourself."

"You're right. Every time I hear a car drive down the street, I think it's the police coming to arrest me," I said and sighed, laying down my fork. "It's ridiculous. I didn't do anything."

"Plenty of innocent people go to jail every day. It's wise to try to find the killer. Plus, it could be kind of fun," she said and grinned.

"Lucy, it's not that fun. I'm not sleeping," I blurted out. I hadn't meant to tell her. I wasn't having nightmares, but I just lay awake at night, staring at the ceiling, mulling over what might happen to me if the police did try to pin Henry's murder on me.

"Oh, I'm sorry, Allie. Maybe you should get some help?" she said, reaching across the table and putting her hand on the back of mine.

"No, I'll get through it. I just need some time. And maybe I need to put in some longer runs. You know, to wear myself out," I said and picked up my fork and took a bite of my pie. My heart wasn't in it, but there it was, sitting in front of me.

"I have an idea," Lucy said, brightening. "We need more evidence. Right now I'm putting my money on Charles, but maybe we're overlooking something."

"And how are we going to get more evidence?" I asked.

"Easy. We'll break into the restaurant and take a look around for ourselves."

I stared at her. "Are you crazy? Break into the restaurant? We could go to jail for that."

"You could go to jail for a murder you didn't commit," she countered.

She had a point. One that had me more and more worried with each passing day. But I had never lived a life of crime. It seemed wrong to start one so late in life.

AT MIDNIGHT WE WERE creeping along the back of Henry's Home Cooking Restaurant. At Lucy's insistence, we had donned all black. My yoga pants were finally coming in handy, and we wore black ski masks so it would be harder to see us in the dark. I mean, we wouldn't look suspicious if we were pulled over by the police on the way over, right?

"Check that window," Lucy whispered.

I reached up and tried to shove the window open. No go. "What if the place has a burglar alarm? Or cameras?" I whispered, following Lucy around the corner.

"No chance. Henry was too cheap," she tossed over her shoulder.

"Well, how are we going to get in?" The place looked like it was locked up pretty tight. Henry's widow hadn't opened the restaurant since he died. I didn't blame her. If it were me, I couldn't bear to be in the place my husband had spent so much time when he was alive.

She stopped at the back door and looked at me with a grin. The moonlight glinted off her white teeth. "I came prepared," she said, holding up a small canvas bag.

"What is that?" I asked, leaning over to look into it when she opened it.

"My bag of tricks," she said, rummaging around inside of it. She pulled out a small silver tool and a thin piece of wire. "I was a Girl Scout. Always be prepared was our motto."

"That was the Boy Scouts' motto," I pointed out. "Do you have any idea what you're doing?"

"Please. Of course, I know what I'm doing," she said, kneeling on the ground and sticking the wire and the tool into the doorknob. The moon was full and provided a little light, but it was hard for me to see what she was doing.

"Do you have a flashlight on your phone?" she asked, looking up at me.

I pulled my phone out and turned it on. "Someone's going to see this light."

"I'll hurry," she said, jiggling the wire in the keyhole.

"What is that thing?"

"A bobby pin."

"Where did you learn this?" I asked. It didn't look like she was making any progress, and I was doubting her skills at this point.

"The internet," she said, still jiggling.

"Seriously? Won't everyone know how to pick locks now?" I asked. "Seems kind of dumb to advertise that kind of thing."

"I don't know. Maybe. Who cares as long as we can get this door open?"

She was starting to get cranky. It was chilly, and my nose was on the verge of running. I kept looking over my shoulder, expecting to see a police car pull up. I hoped she was right about there being no alarm system.

She worked and worked on the lock, and after nearly thirty minutes I was just about to tell her we needed to go, when she cried, "Aha!"

"Shh!" I said, looking around to make sure no one had heard her.

"After you, madam," she said, pushing the back door open.

"Well, it's about time," I said and entered the restaurant.

"Stop your complaining. You couldn't do any better," she said, following behind me.

I shined the light from my phone around the room and stopped at the place on the floor where I had last seen Henry's body. I let out a breath I didn't know I was holding. The place smelled of pine cleaner, and the floor was spotless.

"Cleanest place in town," Lucy said. "I wonder if Henry's widow is a germaphobe too?"

I flashed my phone around the room, checking for security cameras. It looked like Lucy was right about Henry being too cheap to buy them. I just hoped there wasn't a nanny cam inside a head of lettuce somewhere.

"What exactly are we looking for?" I asked. "This place has been wiped clean, and I'm sure the police have been over and over it."

"I don't know," she said, opening the door to the industrial-sized silver refrigerator.

"Don't you think the police would have found anything worth finding?" I asked, peering over her shoulder. The restaurant may have been spotless, but the food inside of the refrigerator hadn't been touched and the stink of rotting food wafted out. "Pee-yew."

"Police don't know everything. They might have missed a big clue," she said. "I heard Henry's widow was going to re-open the restaurant next week."

"Really," I answered. "She better get this thing cleaned out then." There was a package of rotting steak sitting front and center in the refrigerator. The milk looked curdled, the lettuce was forming a puddle of brown slime beneath it, and a pink Pyrex bowl full of who knows what was still in there. This thing would need airing out if the restaurant were to open next week.

"You're right about that." Lucy slammed the door shut. "Disgusting."

Other than the interior of the refrigerator, the kitchen was spotless. I wondered if Martha had been called in to help clean. From the smell of it, it had been done earlier in the day. No, I thought. There's no way Martha would come back in here after what she had seen. After what we had both seen. I was an idiot for being here now. It was giving me the willies, and I was ready to be done with this adventure. I hoped there was no such thing as ghosts and that Henry wouldn't make an appearance.

I opened and closed a few drawers, but all they had in them were a few kitchen utensils. Not nearly as many as I would have thought a restaurant kitchen would have. A cork bulletin board hung on one wall, and I went over to investigate. I shined the light on the papers that were stuck on it. Mostly recipes and the gas bill. An employee schedule hung on a clipboard. The recipes were on yellowed and stained paper. Grandma's old-fashioned oatmeal cookies recipe was a print off from the local newspaper from 1974. I wondered whose grandma had supplied the recipe.

"Where's his office?" Lucy asked after she had searched all the cupboards.

I led the way, shining the light on the floor, hoping it wasn't visible from the outside. The door to Henry's office was open, and we stepped inside. Lucy flipped on the light, and I protested.

"There's no window in here," she said, heading toward Henry's makeshift desk.

I closed the door. "The light might shine down the hallway and still be visible through the outer windows." I headed toward a file cabinet and slid a drawer open. As clean as Henry was, he sure had his paperwork in a mess. I riffled through the files. It looked like Henry held on to every receipt he had ever gotten.

"Hmm," I said when I found a file in the back with suspicious-looking slips of paper in it.

"What is it?" Lucy asked. She was digging through the small wastepaper basket near the desk.

"I think these are, I don't know, betting slips?" I said, holding one up for inspection. "I've never seen one, but it has names and numbers on it. And I think that's a race track name." I had never bet on anything in my life, but from the size of the file, it looked like Henry had bet on a lot of things.

Lucy got up and came to take a look. "It is a betting slip," Lucy said, taking the piece of paper from me. "I wonder if he owed someone money?"

I looked at her. "Maybe he did, and that's why he couldn't give Charles a raise. And maybe he couldn't pay his bookie, and he killed him over it." That seemed like a fair explanation. No one in Sandy Harbor would just kill someone for no reason.

"I think you're on to something," Lucy said. We looked at each other in silence, thinking this over.

"How do we find out who his bookie was?" I finally asked.

"I dunno. How do you know where to place a bet if you wanted to do that? We need to be the bettor to figure this out," she said.

I stood up and accidentally knocked a glass ashtray off the top of the filing cabinet. It made a heavy thud when it hit the carpet. We both screamed and then looked at each other wide-eyed. "Shh," I said and tried to listen to see if anyone had heard us.

The ashtray was made of heavy amber glass and didn't break when it hit the carpet. Who still had ashtrays around? I couldn't remember ever smelling smoke on Henry. It looked like something from the 1970s.

"It's a clue," Lucy said, reading my mind.

I narrowed my eyes at the ashtray. "Maybe Henry's bookie smokes, and he kept it here for their meetings."

"So we need to find someone that smokes and looks suspicious," Lucy said.

"I guess we could go around town smelling everyone that looks suspicious," I said.

"Thanks to the cigarette tax, hardly anyone smokes anymore," Lucy agreed. "It can't be that hard to narrow it down."

Things were starting to get crazy. First, we had broken and entered, and now we were going to go around sniffing suspicious-looking people.

"We need to go," I said. "And I'm taking this with me." I picked up the file, and we headed out the back door, being careful to leave everything else the way it was when we got there.

I LAY IN BED THAT NIGHT, going through the file we had taken. It looked like Henry loved to play the horses. And place football bets. Plus a few others that were so vague, I wasn't sure what they were. Sometimes the bets were small, fifty or a hundred dollars, but on more than a few occasions, they were for several thousand dollars. Those were mostly horse racing bets.

I came across one that had the initials RH on it in handwriting and a brief note that said pay 8/23 and the amount $10,899. Had Henry placed a large bet and lost? Or did someone owe him money? Maybe he was a bookie on the side, and he had put pressure on RH to pay up, and RH took exception to it.

I sighed. There wasn't a lot of information to go on. I wondered if the racetrack kept track of bets placed? It seemed like they would have to. But what difference did it make if they did? I was sure they wouldn't just hand out information like that.

Was it illegal to place bets through a bookie instead of directly at the track? I had no idea. I had lived a rather safe, mundane life and had no idea how to do illegal things. Well, up until this evening, anyway. Now I was officially a criminal. But I wasn't going to spread that tidbit of information around.

I would have to think about this and figure something out.
Maybe Lucy would have some ideas.

Chapter Thirteen

I had just stepped out of the shower and was in my bathrobe when the doorbell rang. I quickly wrapped a towel around my wet hair and trotted over to the door and peered through the peephole. I pushed air out between my teeth when I saw it was Detective Blanchard.

"Who is it?" I said, annoyed.

"I'm pretty sure you can see who it is," he answered.

"I'm not dressed, so I can't open the door," I called back. This guy was getting on my nerves. Why did he need to stop by unannounced like this?

"I'll wait," he said.

I scowled. Who did he think he was? It was still early, and I had already answered all of his questions. Then I remembered that Lucy and I broke into Henry's Home Cooking Restaurant. My heart jumped in my chest, and I pushed the thought away. We were careful, and Henry was too cheap to put up cameras. There was no way he knew what we had done.

"I'll be right out," I called and headed back to my bedroom.

I quickly put on underclothes and then threw on a sweatshirt over a pair of jeans. I tried to drag my feet and make him wait, but the idea of an authority figure, albeit an annoying authority figure, standing on my front porch made me move faster. I took the towel off and ran my fingers through my hair. Darn him. I wasn't company presentable, and he knew it.

I returned to the front door and opened it for him, still feeling a little naked without makeup. "Can I help you?" I said, trying to stay as neutral as I could.

"May I come in?" he asked. He was dressed more casually today, in a pair of dress slacks and a pullover sweater that accented his broad shoulders. I could smell his aftershave, and it gave me a pinch of emotion. My husband had always worn aftershave, regardless of whether he was going out or not. I had loved that about him. Even after a workout, he had always managed to smell good.

I took a step back and let him in. Part of me wanted to refuse, but again, the thought of orange jumpsuits and silver bracelets danced through my mind.

"Thank you. I appreciate your cooperation," he said as I led him to the living room. I wondered if the threat of jail time was behind that word, cooperation.

"Can I get you some coffee?" I reluctantly offered.

"No, thank you, I just had a question for you," he said and took a seat on the sofa.

I sat down across from him on the loveseat. "Yes?"

He narrowed his eyes at me and leaned forward. "It seems that someone was snooping around Henry's Home Cooking Restaurant last night. You wouldn't happen to know anything about it, would you?"

My heart stopped. When it started up again, it nearly exploded in my chest. There was no beating around the bush with this guy. I was pretty sure my face had turned ghost white.

"Well—why would you think I would know something about that?" I clasped my hands together in my lap to keep them from shaking.

"Just a hunch," he said, staring me down.

I forced myself to breathe. He had no proof it was Lucy and me, or he would have arrested me first thing. "I have no idea what you're talking about. Are you accusing me of breaking and entering?" There. That would put him on the defensive.

"No, I am not accusing you," he said, sitting back a bit.

"Why would you even ask me?" I said, feeling more confident now. "I'm not capable of breaking into a building. Was there damage done to the building? I wouldn't know the first thing about breaking into a building. I can't imagine people doing things like that. Who in their right mind would do that?" I bit my lip to make myself stop talking.

His lips pressed together tightly. "No, no damage was done to the building. But there were some things moved around. Possibly some missing items. That sort of thing."

It was my turn to be suspicious. Lucy and I had been careful, and we hadn't taken anything that would have been noticeable. If the police knew about the betting slips, then they would have taken them, assuming they were evidence. But if they weren't evidence, then why would they notice they were gone? "What kind of missing things?" I had to know.

"Oh, maybe a file or two," he said, sitting back on the couch. "And there was something knocked on the floor that hadn't been there before. Back in Henry's office."

The ashtray. Hadn't we picked it up? I tried to keep my eyes from going wide, but I was pretty sure I failed. "Well, it could have been the cleaning lady. I heard Henry's widow is going to reopen the restaurant next week. Surely she had cleaning people in there."

He nodded slowly. "I suppose that could have happened. But the cleaning people came in first thing yesterday morning, and I was in there yesterday afternoon. I also spoke with Charles Allen again. He said you accused him of being the killer. But he thinks you're the killer."

"What? He said what? That liar! I only wanted to make sure he was okay after our traumatizing experience, and of course, I wondered if he knew of anyone that might have something against Henry. Being his employee, I would think he would have noticed something," I said, defending myself.

"I see," he said and leaned forward again. "Allie, it's a really big mistake for you to get involved in this investigation in any way. You need to leave it to the professionals. If you did decide to break into the restaurant, I'm not saying that you did, mind you, but if you did, then you could go to jail. And you're too pretty for jail."

I swallowed hard, taking this in, and then opened my mouth to speak. Wait. What? Did he say I was pretty? I felt color go to my cheeks. "I assure you, Detective, I am not investigating anything."

He looked at me a few moments before speaking. "Good. I don't want to have to arrest you or your friend. Now if you'll excuse me, I've got to get going." With that, he got up and showed himself to the door. I followed him to the door and watched him drive away.

What was it with that man? First, he practically accuses me of murder. And then he calls me pretty. Last week someone told him that I argued with Henry the night before he died. I had assumed it was Charles. Maybe I was wrong, but if I was, who else could it have been? And why didn't he accuse me of murder then, assuming it was Charles he had spoken to?

Chapter Fourteen

The more I thought about it, the angrier I got as I pushed my buggy down the cereal aisle of Shaw's Market. The nerve of Detective Blanchard thinking I would break into Henry's Home Cooking Restaurant. Never mind that I had. But I did not have the face of a criminal. And it's not like I did it for personal gain. No. I was helping him solve the case. When I found the killer, I was going to demand an apology.

I picked up a box of raisin bran, on sale for $2.50, and tossed it in the buggy. I needed to talk to Lucy about this. We needed to be more careful. And who notices one ashtray on the floor, anyway? And the files? Had he counted the files to know how many there were? That file cabinet had been in a mess, and I couldn't imagine anyone knowing that a file was missing unless they had counted.

By the time I turned the corner and headed down the bread aisle, I was steaming. I looked up and saw Charles Allen looking over the English muffins, and I headed right for him.

"Charles Allen, you are a despicable human being," I said through clenched teeth and stopped the buggy just short of his sizable backside.

"What?" he said, looking over his shoulder. His eyes got big when he saw me. "What do you want?"

"You told Detective Blanchard that I accused you of murder, and I did no such thing. Lucy did. Now he thinks I'm a suspicious person. And after I baked you that pie. Why, you should be ashamed of yourself." I gripped the buggy handle tightly.

"What? No, I didn't do that, I swear, Allie," he said and turned around to face me. My buggy was so close to him, it was difficult for him to do turn, so he took tiny steps and eased his large body around.

"He said you did, and I am inclined to believe him," I said. "I have never done one thing wrong in my life, and now you accuse me of murder?" Okay, I had done one thing wrong. Actually, I'd done a lot of things wrong, but that wasn't the point.

"No... no, see, I think he misunderstood. I said that we had a discussion, but I never said you were the murderer." He shifted from one foot to the other and glanced to the right and then to the left.

I gripped the buggy handle. "You had better not be going around pointing the finger of blame at me, Charles Allen." I glanced over my shoulder. People were looking in our direction. I turned and narrowed my eyes at him.

"Oh, I'm not, I swear," he said holding his right hand up to swear he was telling the truth. His black hair fell across his forehead, and he pushed it back with his other hand.

"I think you know who did it, and that's why you're trying to cast suspicion on me," I hissed.

"What? No, I have no idea who did it," he hissed back.

"Then where were you on the night of the murder? Where were you really? Because I don't believe for one minute that you were visiting your mother. You don't strike me as the sentimental type," I accused. "And where did you get the money to pay for such a nice house on a fry cook's pay? Answer me that."

His mouth opened, closed, and opened again. His face turned red, and I thought he was having a heart attack. "Chef! I am a chef! And for your information, I didn't earn that money from my chef job," he sputtered.

"Oh? And where did you earn that money?" I could be mean when I wanted to be. I'm not proud of it, but the gift does come in handy occasionally.

"I uh, well, it's like this," he said, looking to the right and then to the left again. People had wandered out of the bread aisle, most likely in search of a manager to break up something that could very possibly end up in a brawl.

He leaned toward me, and there was the faint smell of sweat. "I have this gig on the weekends," he said, and then took another look both ways down the aisle. "I sing on the weekends."

I took a step back, mostly from the smell, but partly from this tidbit of information. I had never heard that Charles was a singer. "You sing? Where?"

He breathed out through his mouth. "At the Coastal Heights hotel over in Bangor. I'm an Elvis impersonator." When he said Elvis impersonator, he looked quickly over each shoulder again. He sure was a nervous Nellie.

I stared at him. Had I heard him right? "A what?"

He rolled his eyes. "An Elvis impersonator," he whispered.

When that sunk in, I threw my head back and laughed. I couldn't help myself.

"Yeah, you laugh it up, but I make good money doing it. And I'm good at it," he said, turning redder.

"Oh, I'm sorry, Charles, but do you expect me to believe that?" I wasn't sure if he was telling the truth or not, but it was a good joke, either way.

"I don't care if you believe it or not. I sing at the Coastal Heights hotel every weekend. That's why I stayed at the restaurant. Henry was always good about allowing me to have weekends off. I got to use my cooking skills during the week, and on weekends I got to use my singing skills. It was a win-win situation."

He looked like he was telling the truth, but murderers were probably good liars. I was almost sure of it.

"Fine, Charles. Whatever. I'm sure Detective Blanchard will be checking out your alibi. But you better not tell him that I murdered Henry ever again."

"Yeah, yeah, I didn't do it in the first place, but I won't ever say it, I promise."

I stared him down for a minute and then whipped the buggy around and headed for the checkout. I felt all eyes on me, but I didn't care. I was innocent.

WHEN I GOT HOME, I Googled the Coastal Heights hotel. I clicked on the entertainment tab and read about all the shows they offered. There was an Elvis impersonator, and I clicked to enlarge the picture. I squinted my eyes and examined it, but it was hard to tell if it was Charles. This Elvis wore a white jumpsuit with sparkles all over it, and it was hard to imagine

Charles squeezing into that, but it could have been him. I slid my desk drawer open and pulled out a magnifying glass and took a closer look. It did look like him. Charles certainly had the hair for it. I sighed and put the magnifying glass down. I was sure that Detective Blanchard would be checking to make sure he was really there that night. I could call him and double-check, but I was pretty sure I would get a lecture on not investigating the murder. It looked like it was back to the drawing board.

I sat back and turned my thoughts to a new blog article. I needed to get one written, and I didn't seem to have any new ideas. I had been writing on grief for so long that sometimes it did feel like I might be living too close to the memories. I had tried to come up with ideas to start a new blog, but I always came up empty-handed. Besides, I felt like I handled the subject of grief sensitively. And from my reader responses, they all seemed to have various family members that didn't handle their grief sensitively, and I felt like I filled a place in their lives.

I opened another tab and went to my blog. There was a notification of new comments. I began reading through them. Three were spam. Another was a grandmother that wrote me frequently. She had lost her son three years ago, and it felt like she was lonely and needed someone to talk to. Another young mother had lost her husband almost a year ago, and she was coming up on the first anniversary of his death. I sighed. If I stopped blogging on grief, where would these people turn?

My breath caught in my throat as I read the last comment.

I know what you did. You may have the police fooled, but I'm not fooled. You murdered Henry Hoffer. You won't get away with it. I'll make sure of that. Sweet dreams.

When my heart finally started beating again, I took a deep breath. The comments didn't go live unless I approved them, so thankfully no one else had seen it. Somebody was trying to set me up to take the fall for Henry's murder. Only the killer would leave a message like that. And the killer knew who I was.

Chapter Fifteen

After reading the comment on my blog from the murderer, I lay down to take a nap. But my mind churned with worry, so all I accomplished was messing up my hair and wrinkling my clothes. After nearly an hour, I sat up and swung my legs over the side of the bed and stared at my feet. I needed a pedicure. Running was hard on the toes.

Then it hit me. RH was Ralph Henderson. The RH from the betting slips we had found in Henry's office. Only that didn't make sense because Ralph was a gardener and not a bookie. Unless Henry was the bookie and he kept a record of what his customers were betting. But if Henry had been a bookie, why not do that full-time? It seemed like in the movies bookies always had money, and Henry would have made more money being a bookie than he did running the restaurant.

Dixie jumped up on the bed and rubbed his head against my arm. I scratched his forehead, deep in thought. I needed to have another chat with Ralph. How did we know he was really fishing? It was convenient that he was by himself. Was it safe to go out on the ocean by yourself? Seemed safer to have someone with you in case of an accident.

I picked up my cell phone from the bedside table and searched for Henderson Gardening Service. In less than five minutes, I had an appointment for gardening service for that afternoon. I had already used the weed eater on my tiny front yard two days earlier, but I needed to speak to Ralph right away and didn't have time to let the grass grow taller. He hadn't been friendly or forthcoming when Lucy and I had spoken to him previously, but maybe he would be a bit more forthcoming if there was the prospect of earning some money. I hadn't given him my last name when I set up the appointment, so I was sure he would show.

RALPH PULLED UP TO the curb with his enclosed trailer full of gardening equipment behind his truck. I stood on the steps waiting for him. My yard was fairly spotless and weed-free. The cooler weather had brought on slower lawn growth, but a couple of my trees had already begun to drop their orange-colored fall leaves. He could break out the leaf blower and tidy up for me.

"Afternoon," he said, getting out of his truck. His forced smile turned to a frown when he recognized me.

I smiled real big. "Good afternoon, Ralph. I'm so glad you could make it on such short notice."

"Yeah, I had a cancellation," he said and slammed the truck door harder than was necessary. He glanced around at my yard. "Don't seem like you need much done here."

"Well, there are all these leaves," I said, motioning toward the obvious. "Oh, and you know, I think I'd like some nice fall flowers in the planter in front of the house." The weather would soon take a cold turn, and the flowers wouldn't last long, but maybe they would survive until mid-October. It didn't matter. I didn't care about flowers, anyway. I wouldn't argue with him about flower colors, either. That may have been Henry's downfall.

He made a snorting noise and swung open my little gate and walked into the yard. My yard was enclosed with a darling white picket fence that had scallops along the top. It set off my creamy yellow cottage perfectly.

"I guess I could do that. You got much of a backyard?"

"Just a small one, but that probably needs some work, too. Follow me," I said and led him around the side and reached over the gate and unlatched it.

He followed me into the backyard. The grass was still green and closely cropped. I had put in new rose bushes the previous spring, and they were still blooming.

He snorted. "Looks like whoever has been doing your yard has done a pretty good job. I don't know why you called me."

"Well that would be me, but I'm really not a yard person, so that's why I called you. I would love to be relieved of yard duty," I said and laughed, trying to keep things light and friendly. He stared blankly back at me. That Ralph was a card, I tell ya.

"I'll write up a proposal," he said and turned back toward the gate.

"Ralph, I have a question for you," I said. Then I realized that I was with a possible killer in my backyard. A backyard that had a solid eight-feet high wood fence that no one could see over.

He turned slowly toward me and looked at me without saying a word.

I swallowed. "Let's go out front, shall we?" It would have been far too easy for him to pull out a knife and do to me what he may have done to Henry.

He followed me around front without a word. At the front walk, I turned toward him. "Were you really out fishing the night of Henry's murder?"

His face clouded over in anger. "Is that what this is about? You're wasting my time when I could be working and earning money for my kids?"

"Oh no, not at all. I really do want to hire a gardener, and you were the first one I thought of," I said, trying to smooth things over. "It's just that the police are having such a hard time finding Henry's killer."

"And you think it's me?" he said, his voice getting louder. "Lady, you are crazy. I don't have time for this."

I've been called that before.

"Am I, Ralph?" I said and whipped out the piece of paper I had tucked into my hoodie pocket earlier. I held it out to him so he could see it. "You owed Henry Hoffer money, and I think you killed him when he tried to collect." My heart was pounding in my chest, and I glanced around to see if there were any witnesses, just in case Ralph decided to shut me up permanently. The street was empty, and I silently cursed my timing.

Ralph took three steps toward me and grabbed the paper out of my hand. He looked it over, and his face turned the color of beets. "Listen, you don't have any idea what you're talking about. I already told you where I was."

He tossed the paper on the ground and stormed back to his truck. Jumping into his truck, he slammed the door nearly off the hinges. He shot one last angry look at me and started the engine. His tires left rubber on the street when he pulled away.

He didn't even give me an estimate.

Chapter Sixteen

"I think there's someone you should investigate," I said, sitting across from Detective Blanchard. He had a small office at the nearly empty police station. A small desk sat facing the door, and there were two folding metal visitors' chairs in front of the desk. I guess the Sandy Harbor police department wasn't fancy.

He sat and looked at me without saying a word. He had the prettiest blue eyes framed in long dark lashes that I had ever seen. I couldn't tell if he was mad or if he just wanted me to disappear. After a few moments had passed, I decided he really just wanted me to disappear.

"Well? Aren't you going to ask me who?" I asked when he remained silent. My handbag was in my lap, and I held it there. The floor didn't look very clean.

I had hurried right over to the police station after Ralph left my house. I didn't want to waste any time in case he had gone home to plan my murder and would be back this evening to carry it out.

"Sure. Go ahead and tell me who you suspect," the detective said much too calmly, folding his hands on the desk.

I sat up straighter and leaned forward. "Ralph Henderson."

He didn't blink an eye, only continued looking at me.

"Aren't you going to ask me why I suspect him?" I asked.

"Why do you suspect him?" he asked.

He was beginning to bug me. Clearly, I bored him. "Because Henry Hoffer was a bookie and Ralph Henderson made a bad bet that he didn't have the money to pay for. I think."

"Where did you get this information?" he asked, still not looking interested.

I pulled out the file I had taken from Henry's restaurant and laid it on the desk. It's funny, but until that moment, I hadn't thought about the fact that I had stolen the file the night Lucy and I had broken into the restaurant. The same break-in I had denied had ever occurred. I had just laid the evidence of that little crime on his desk in front of him. I forced myself to smile and looked him in the eye like nothing was amiss.

He slowly reached for the file and opened it up and began leafing through the papers. Then he looked at me again. "How did you come by this file?"

I looked at a picture hanging on the wall behind him. "My, that is a nice picture of a sunset."

"Allie, I asked you where you got this file," he said, not even looking at the picture.

"A little bird gave it to me."

He sighed, closing the file folder. "Well, you might tell that little bird that breaking and entering, and burglary, are very serious crimes."

"I did not burgle anything," I protested.

"Taking something that doesn't belong to you is burglary when you break and enter," he informed me, opening the file again and looking through it.

"Well, I didn't do it," I said. "But I think you need to investigate Ralph."

"I'm not seeing anything that points to Ralph Henderson," he said.

I reached over and pulled out the paper that had the initials RH on it. "See? Those are his initials."

"Those could be anyone's initials," he pointed out. "This doesn't prove anything."

"Plus, he has a very bad temper," I said, grasping at proverbial straws. "I mean, he loses it super fast. Within seconds."

"That doesn't mean anything. Many people have short fuses, and I would imagine having someone accuse them of a crime they probably didn't commit would make anyone angry. Did you accuse Ralph Henderson of a crime?"

I swallowed. "Well, he said he was fishing, but of course he was fishing by himself, so he has no alibi," I pointed out.

"Fishing by oneself is not a crime. Not like some other crimes I can think of."

I stared at him. Was he trying to be difficult, or did it just come naturally? "Well, I guess if you want to split hairs."

For a moment he looked like he was trying to suppress a smile. "And besides, these are receipts. Henry Hoffer was the one making the bets," he explained. "Ralph is a gardener. If he were a bookie, he wouldn't need to garden."

My eyes went to the receipt. "Well, you won't know everything until you go and talk to him," I sputtered, beginning to feel flustered. I had been so sure that Henry was the bookie. "But how do you know for sure that Henry wasn't the bookie?"

"I just explained that to you. And I want to warn you, Allie. You are treading on dangerous ground here. You committed a crime to get this information, and then you stole it. There's no way this would ever hold up in court now," he said, leveling his gaze at me.

"Well, if I hadn't done that, then we wouldn't have this information," I protested.

"We might have had this information if you had left the file alone so that I could have had access to it. I think we might be able to add obstruction of justice to the list of crimes you've committed."

I swallowed hard. "I was only trying to help," I whimpered.

"We're dealing with a murderer," he said, softening. "You're putting yourself in danger."

"Well, I wouldn't need to do that if you weren't trying to hang this murder on me," I defended.

"I assure you, I am not trying to hang a murder on anyone. I'm simply trying to do my job and take a murderer off the streets," he said, closing the file again.

"Well, I'm not a murderer," I said, clutching my handbag tightly to my chest.

"Probably not. But I still have to do my job," he pointed out.

"Fine. Do your job then," I answered, sticking my lower lip out a little.

He sighed again. I knew I was trying his patience, but I couldn't help it. I needed to clear my name.

"I will certainly do my best," he said.

"And you'll talk to Ralph Henderson?"

He eyed me. "Only if you promise not to interfere with the case and that you won't steal any more evidence."

I smiled. "Deal."

Chapter Seventeen

"This. Seriously. Sucks." Lucy gasped out each word.

"You'll get used to it," I said evenly as we jogged slowly along the running path. I had finally talked her into coming along with me. It was the raisin apple sour cream pie that finally did it. She had over-indulged and gained four pounds overnight. I was going to point out that it was impossible to gain that much in one night but thought better of it when she volunteered to run with me. At the pace we were going, I would have to run again after I dropped her off at her house so I could get a real run in. It was fine, though. I was happy to have the company.

"Well, it seriously sucks," she said, slowing to a walk and breathing hard.

"It takes a while to get used to it, but it will get easier," I said. "The benefits are so worth it."

"Do you think Detective Blanchard will interrogate Ralph?" she asked through gasps. I had filled her in on my findings on the way to the running trail.

"I certainly hope so. He has such a bad temper, I'm sure he's the murderer," I said, taking a swig from my water bottle.

"You should have had me there for backup. That was dangerous."

"I know, but I wanted to get the information as soon as possible, and I knew you were working at the time." I also thought she might get a little wild with the accusations once Ralph got there. I had wanted to try to get information out of Ralph, not that it turned out that way. But she was right. With Ralph's temper, it was a risk to do what I did. I agreed with her on that.

"Hey, is that that handsome detective over there?" she said, pointing to a lone figure coming toward us. He was running along at what looked like a good clip, head held high with good form.

"Maybe," I said. I wasn't sure if Detective Blanchard was a runner.

We walked along so Lucy could catch her breath, and the runner headed toward us. As he got closer, I thought it did look like the detective.

When he got close to us, he slowed to a walk.

"Good morning, Detective," Lucy sang out.

I rolled my eyes. She seemed to be overlooking the fact that this man was still trying to hang a murder on me, and if he felt like it, he could also charge me with the laundry list of crimes he had accused me of the previous day.

"Good morning," he replied. I noticed he wasn't breathing very hard and that he appeared to be in good shape. He looked at me and nodded his greeting.

"Good morning. Did you get a chance to speak to Ralph Henderson?" I asked. No use beating around the bush. We all knew it was the question I wanted answered.

He glanced at Lucy and then turned back to me. "Indeed I did. Turns out he wasn't fishing at all."

"I knew it!" I gloated.

"Turns out he was at the hospital, watching his baby being born," he said looking very serious.

"What? That doesn't make sense," I said, my face falling at the news. "Why would he lie and say he was fishing?"

"Wait a minute, I know Ralph's wife from the bank. She's older than I am. No way was she having a baby," Lucy said, pointing at the detective. "He's lying. He has no alibi, and he committed the murder." She looked at me, nodding.

"Yeah, it's just like I said," I told him, returning to my gloating. I wanted justice, and I wanted it now.

"That's correct. Ralph Henderson's wife did not have a baby," he said just as seriously as he said everything else. I wondered if this guy even had a sense of humor. He certainly never showed it if he did.

"What do you mean?" I asked, confused. And then it dawned on me. "Seriously?"

He nodded. "Sorry to burst your bubble, but Ralph was not the killer."

"Well, do you know this for sure? He could be lying," I said, feeling dejected.

"I know this for sure," he said confidently.

"I don't get it," Lucy said, eyebrows furrowed.

"So that's why he left his gardening equipment in front of the restaurant?" I asked.

He nodded smugly. "He was in a hurry. He didn't want to miss the birth."

"Well, what other leads do you have?" I asked. "Is there a person of interest?" I had to know that I wasn't that person of interest. I wasn't sure if he would tell me or not, though. He wasn't one to talk much.

"I can't divulge that kind of information," he said, giving me a level gaze. "And I want to repeat my warning about not getting involved in the investigation."

He sure was bossy. I put my hands on my hips. "I got it already."

"Do I make myself clear?" he said to Lucy. He gave Lucy the eye, but she was still trying to figure things out.

"Huh? Yeah, sure," she said. "I wish I knew what was going on here."

"Good. I'm sure I'll be seeing you ladies around," he said and took off down the trail in the same direction he had been going.

"Oh, I get it now," Lucy said. "Ol' Ralph had someone on the side."

I rolled my eyes and started walking. "I can't imagine who it would be."

"Some women are desperate," she said, following after me.

"I guess that explains why he got so mad when I questioned him about that night," I said. "He didn't want anyone to know what he's been up to."

"It's kind of neat, really," Lucy said, taking a drink from her water bottle.

"Neat? How so?" I asked, turning to look at her.

"Well, one soul was lost that night, but another one came into the world. Oh, do you believe in reincarnation? Maybe that baby is Henry!"

"Oh, Lucy, please. That's a fairy tale. I don't believe in reincarnation," I said. "I guess it's back to the drawing board."

"Yeah, but who else could have done it? I wonder if Ralph would have had enough time to commit the murder and then get back to the hospital in time for the baby to be born? Labor can go on forever. He might have had plenty of time," she said.

"Maybe. But you know Detective Blanchard isn't going to answer any more questions where Ralph is concerned," I said. "We'll just have to go back over what we already know and try to figure this out. I'll check out that Elvis show Charles said he was putting on. He might have had time to get back and do the deed, or he could have done it earlier in the evening."

This all was very worrying. If the other two suspects were cleared, then that left me. And I didn't have an alibi.

Chapter Eighteen

Henry's Home Cooking Restaurant re-opened on Wednesday, and I decided to drop by. I was curious as to how business would be now that everyone knew a murder was committed there. I pulled into the parking lot, and the place was packed. I should have known. Sandy Harbor was a small town, and everyone wanted to know all the gruesome details. The Alabama town I had grown up in was a little bigger than Sandy Harbor, and it was the same there. Everyone wanted to know all the gossip.

I could still smell pine cleaner when I entered the restaurant. Maybe the smell was permanent now. Most of the booths were filled, as well as most of the tables. Glancing around, I notice the majority of customers only had coffee or sodas in front of them. It figured. They were probably all wondering how they could get a tour of the kitchen.

I was surprised to see Henry's widow working the cash register. She had a smile on her face and was chatting with people as she took their payments. She seemed incredibly relaxed and happy. Hmm... maybe I had overlooked a suspect. If my husband had been murdered, the last place I would want to be was the scene of the crime. I also wouldn't want to answer questions from the town's nosy Nellies.

I went to her. "Good morning, Cynthia, how are you doing?"

I saw a hint of something in her eyes, but she recovered quickly. "I'm well, Allie. How are you?"

"Good. I just wanted to check in on you. I've been thinking about you and saying a few prayers."

She looked grateful. "Oh, thank you so much, Allie. I do appreciate that. I feel kind of lost. I checked out your blog. It's been very helpful."

Now I felt like a heel for wondering if she could be the killer. I smiled. "I'm so glad to hear that. If there's anything I can do for you, let me know, will you? Even if you just want to talk, don't hesitate to call me."

"I may take you up on that, Allie," she said.

She showed me to a table, and I realized I could see Charles in the kitchen through the pass-through from where I sat. He glanced in my direction, and I gave him a small wave. He stopped stirring the pot on the stove in front of him and stared at me. Then he shook his head and looked away.

I knew what I wanted, but I looked over the menu anyway. When I heard a familiar voice, I looked up from the menu to see Martha Newberry standing near the register talking to Cynthia. Tucked under her arm was something pink. I wondered if she had cleaned this morning, and I also wondered who had cleaned up the blood in the kitchen. I shuddered. Did Martha have it in her to continue working here after what she had seen the morning of Henry's death? I know I wouldn't.

Eileen Smith took my order, and I played on my phone until my food arrived. I had a notification of comments left on my blog, so I signed in to read them. There were a couple of nice notes from people I didn't know and one from the woman coming up on the first anniversary of her husband's death. I was glad I could help people feel better at a time when things were so difficult for them.

My heart stopped when I read the last comment.

Don't think you'll get away with what you did. Justice will prevail. And if the justice system doesn't take care of you, I will.

My heart came pounding back to life, and I had to fight for that first breath. *Breathe*, I told myself. I glanced around the restaurant to see if anyone was watching me, but the only person looking in my direction was Martha. She raised a hand to say hello and turned back to Cynthia. I sighed and looked at my phone again. Why would the murderer send me messages like this?

I needed to show these comments to Detective Blanchard. But then, he would question me harder, wouldn't he? He might think that this person knew I was the killer. And if this person knew, or thought they knew, then that might be enough for Detective Blanchard to take a closer look at me. Since I had no real alibi, I couldn't defend myself. Maybe that was what the murderer wanted me to do—tell the detective so it would keep him from looking for the real killer. I wasn't sure what to do now.

I left my breakfast untouched and went to find Lucy. My mind was in a panic and I needed a clear head to help me decide whether I should tell Detective Blanchard about this or not.

Chapter Nineteen

I remembered Lucy was at her part-time job, so I went home and texted her to come over as soon as she got off. I made tea while I waited and watched the hands of the clock make their way around.

I sighed and took another sip of my tea, then set it aside. I needed coffee for this kind of thing. I put a pot on to brew and checked the clock again. What was the murderer's game? He had nothing to win by tormenting me with these comments. I hadn't committed the murder, and I didn't know who did. So why send the comments to me?

I had just poured myself a cup of coffee when the doorbell rang. I nearly jumped out of my skin at the sound of the chimes. Maybe caffeine was the last thing I needed right then.

I went to the door and looked through the peephole before opening it. Martha Newberry stood smiling up at the peephole. I sighed and opened the door.

"Good afternoon, Allie," she said cheerily. "How are you today?"

"I'm fine Martha, how are you?" What was he doing here? I glanced past her, hoping Lucy would be here soon.

"Good, good. May I come in?" She was dressed in a light jacket and had a pink knit hat on her head.

"Of course, where are my manners?" I said, standing back from the door. She scooted her walker through the door. Her pink handbag and the shopping bag I had given her when I gave her the apple pie were in the little basket on the front of the walker. I led her into the living room.

"Oh my, is that freshly brewed coffee? That smells so good," she said and hobbled after me.

"Would you like some?" I asked. Maybe having company while I waited for Lucy would do me some good.

"I would love some coffee. Oh, and I brought you this," she said, motioning toward the shopping bag. "Take it out of the basket, will you?"

"Are you feeling all right, Martha?" She hadn't used the walker when she was in Henry's.

She waved a hand at the walker. "Oh, it's nothing. My hip aches from time to time, and I feel steadier using this old thing."

I smiled and removed the bag from the walker basket. "What is this?"

"Just a little something I whipped up. I'm sure it doesn't compare to that delicious apple pie you made for me, but it's rather tasty if I do say so myself. May I sit down?" she asked and headed for the sofa before I could answer.

"Yes, of course." I reached into the bag and pulled out a pink Pyrex covered dish. Something about it triggered something in my memory, but I couldn't quite put my finger on it. "Why, what is it?"

"It's a bread pudding. The recipe has been in my family for years. Do help yourself. I've just finished a late lunch and couldn't eat another bite, but that coffee smells wonderful. Coffee goes so well with bread pudding, don't you know?"

"That's so sweet of you. I bet it's wonderful," I said and headed to the kitchen with it. I removed the glass lid on the pink bowl. The aroma of cinnamon and vanilla wafted out along with something else I couldn't quite put my finger on. "What is that scent? Do you have a secret ingredient in your bread pudding?" I called from the kitchen. I loved everything to do with baking, and this smelled wonderful. I needed to know her secret.

"Oh yes, indeed I do. Indeed I do," she said and chuckled.

I got a cup out of the cupboard and poured her some coffee. "Cream and sugar?" I called, still trying to put my finger on what the secret ingredient might be.

"Yes, please. Both," she said. "Plenty of cream. My husband used to say that I took a little coffee with my cream." She chuckled.

I knew baking ingredients inside and out. In the South, people sometimes used ingredients that you wouldn't associate with baking, like sour kraut in my mother's super moist chocolate cake. I decided maybe older ladies from the North probably did the same, and Martha's bread pudding must be one of those recipes. I was going to have to pry the recipe out of her because the smell was making my mouth water.

I put cream and sugar and two cups of coffee on a serving tray for us both. It would be nice to have someone to visit with and take my mind off the threats I had been receiving. Martha needed someone to talk to about her late husband, anyway. I had been feeling guilty that I had not followed through on my promise to spend some time with her.

"Thank you, dear," she said with a smile. Her Maine accent was thick, and 'dear' came out sounding like deaya. "You get yourself some of that bread pudding and sit awhile."

"I'm going to do just that," I said and headed back to the kitchen for a bowl of bread pudding. "This smells delicious."

"Oh, it is!" she called. "But it needs to be eaten warm with cream poured over it. The cream brings out the flavor."

I spooned some bread pudding into a bowl and brought it to the living room, sitting on the sofa across from her. I rarely ate in the living room, but I thought it might be more comfortable for her in here. I poured cream over the bread pudding and inhaled. It was heavenly. I looked up and saw she was watching me intently. I put the bowl down and reached for my coffee and added cream and sugar. I felt odd eating in front of my guest, even though she had brought the pudding for me.

"Would you like me to get you a bowl of bread pudding?" I asked.

"No, no. I baked two. One for you and one for me. As I said, I'm much too full from lunch to eat another bite. I'll warm mine up for after supper," she said sweetly.

"How have you been doing, Martha? Are you okay since Henry's murder?" I asked, stirring my coffee.

"Oh yes, I'm fine. It was a start, I'll admit. Such a sad thing," she said, picking up her cup. "Why don't you try the bread pudding, dear?"

I looked down at it. I suddenly didn't feel hungry, and I wasn't sure why. Just then, I burped up a little of the frozen pizza I had nuked and eaten for lunch. "Oh, excuse me. I'm afraid my lunch isn't sitting too well with me."

"Then what you need is something bready like that pudding. It will absorb stomach acids." She smiled at me again and nodded her head.

I wasn't sure I had ever heard anything like that before. "So, what did you put in it? What's your secret ingredient?"

"Only the best ingredients. Real butter, none of that fake stuff, cream, sugar, a very nice brioche, and an assortment of spices. I say if you're going to bother to bake, then use only the best ingredients." She took a sip of her coffee and leaned back.

"I feel the same way," I said and burped again. "Oh dear, I don't know what's gotten into me. I rarely have reflux issues." I got up and trotted to the kitchen. "Sorry, Martha!" I called over my shoulder.

"That's okay, dear. But you're letting your bread pudding cool down."

I swallowed an acid pill and returned to the living room. "That should fix it. I'm afraid I shouldn't eat any of that delicious bread pudding, though. I should let my stomach settle."

"Oh, but you must eat it while it's warm," she said, frowning.

"I think I'll wait a bit. I can warm it in the microwave later."

"Oh, but that won't be the same. You need to eat it now. While it's still warm," she said.

"I'll be careful when I warm it up. I'm sure it will be fine. I can tell from the smell that it's a lovely bread pudding," I reassured her but didn't point out that she was going to re-warm her own bread pudding later this evening. I did feel bad about not eating it right away. We bakers could be particular about our desserts. We needed them to be appreciated.

"No, dear, eat it now," she said firmly.

"I will. In a bit," I said, narrowing my eyes at her. Where had I heard this conversation before, I wondered guiltily.

"No, dear. Right now," Martha insisted, leaning forward on the sofa.

I looked at her evenly. She stared right back at me, not budging. What was with her? Why did she want me to eat it now? I mean, I understood the importance of eating certain desserts warm, but not at the expense of the eater's health.

"Are you going to try it?" she asked, pursing her lips.

"Yes. Later," I answered and smiled. I could be stubborn too.

Martha's eyes got big, and she suddenly tossed her walker aside and sprang to her feet. She produced a large butcher knife from her handbag and lunged at me. "I said, eat it now!"

I screamed and dodged the knife, jumping to the end of the couch. If I hadn't seen it for myself, I would never have believed that little old Martha Newberry could move so quickly. She was beside me in a minute, holding the knife to my throat. "Martha, what are you doing?" I squeaked out. I could feel the sharp blade against my neck.

"I want you to eat that bread pudding. Now. Soon you won't have any stomach issues at all," she said and gave a small chuckle.

"Why are you doing this, Martha?" I squeaked out.

She gave me an eerie smile. "Because you're nosy. Charles told me you had been asking around about Henry's killer. Then Ralph told me the same thing, and that detective has made a couple of visits to my home. If it weren't for you, that detective would have continued thinking it was a robber that killed Henry. He told me so. But you just keep sticking your nose where it doesn't belong. Now you get over there and eat that bread pudding." She took a step back, just enough to let me move over on the sofa. She made a motion with the knife that said I better get moving.

"But why would you kill Henry?" I asked, thinking I might stall for time. "And what's the bread pudding got to do with it?" I thought I knew what it had to do with it, but I needed time to think.

She laughed. "I suppose it doesn't matter if I tell you. Henry killed my Walter. I have thought of nothing but revenge since that day. So I brought him some bread pudding. My special bread pudding. But you had brought an apple pie to him, and he insisted he had eaten pie already and refused to try my bread pudding. So things got ugly. And things will get ugly for you too if you don't eat up. I'd hate to make a mess of your lovely living room. I like your throw rug."

I swallowed hard and remembered the pink Pyrex dish on Henry's countertop. The same pink Pyrex dish that was now sitting on my counter. Martha was crazy. I gave her a weak smile.

"My, Martha, you move much faster than I had imagined you could." I needed a plan, but as long as that huge butcher knife was staring me in the throat, I wasn't sure what that plan would be. Maybe if I rushed her and knocked her down, I wouldn't get more than a little scratch. But Martha had proved remarkably agile for someone her age, and I wasn't sure what other tricks she had up her sleeve.

She laughed again. "You'd be surprised how much lifting weights does for you. When I came home without my Walter that night, I knew I had to do something to occupy my time and keep from feeling depressed. I've been lifting weights and doing yoga ever since. Eventually, I came up with a plan to poison Henry. It was his fault Walter died. I didn't want to do it immediately because someone might suspect me since Walter died at Henry's restaurant. In the meantime, I kept up with the workouts. I feel so much better, you know."

"So were you the one sending me messages on my blog?" I asked, still trying to stall for time.

She nodded. "I took a computer class at the junior college. For research purposes. You were kind enough to give me a business card with your blog address on it, and I decided to have some fun. Now stop stalling."

She was nuts. Bonafide nuts. I reached for the bowl, not sure what I could do at this point. "Martha, you said that Henry killed your husband. How did he do that? I don't remember hearing about a murder." I slowly poured more cream on the bread pudding. May as well make my last meal a good one. I wondered what kind of poison was in it and if it would take long, or if it would hurt.

"By serving him roast beef that was so tough he choked on it. Then he just watched my Walter die instead of helping him," her voice cracked, and she looked near tears. Ordinarily, I would have had sympathy for her, but I decided to keep my sympathy for non-killers.

"Well, perhaps he didn't know how to do the Heimlich maneuver?" I suggested. It seemed reasonable to me.

"Don't you dare take that killer's side of things," she said through gritted teeth. "Now eat!"

I almost snorted at that. She thought it was better that I take her side? Without thinking about it, I threw the bowl of bread pudding in Martha's face. She blocked it with the hand holding the knife and screamed. I slid to the right and jumped to my feet, but Martha was fast, and she knocked me to my knees.

I managed to get a hold of the wrist of her hand holding the knife, but she shoved me, and I lost my balance, falling to the floor. Martha was strong, and taking the knife away from her was proving difficult. We rolled around on the floor between the coffee table and the sofa while I stared at the tip of that knife. I needed room to move, but I was blocked in. I began screaming, hoping the neighbors would hear. I knew the Smiths weren't home, but I was hoping someone would be in hearing range.

"Shut up!" Martha bellowed and put her free hand on my throat and squeezed. She was breathing hard but showed no sign of weakness.

It had to be her non-dominant hand on my throat, but she still had quite a grip. I needed to check into weight lifting. I pulled my head back as far as I could, but I couldn't get away from her. "Let go, Martha!" I squeaked.

"I told you to eat the bread pudding while it was still warm," she said and managed to move her body on top of mine.

I breathed in as deep as I could. Her weight made me feel like I was going to suffocate. "Get off!" I finally forced the words out.

"I don't know why you have to make this so difficult," she panted as she tried to break her knife-wielding hand free from my grip.

I couldn't believe this little old lady was putting up such a fight. "Maybe if you would have read my blog on grief, you could have found a more constructive way of handling things," I suggested when she lost her grip on my throat.

"I'm handling it just fine, dear," she grunted and pulled her knife hand free.

I closed my eyes and screamed as she pulled the knife back and plunged it toward my chest. Suddenly the weight of her body was gone, and I heard her scream.

I opened my eyes and saw Detective Blanchard holding Martha by the scruff of the neck with one hand. His other arm was wrapped around her waist.

"You just calm down, Martha," he said and took a few steps back, still holding onto her.

She screamed again and started crying. "That woman attacked me!" she said, pointing her finger at me.

"What?" I said, coughing and trying to get to my feet. "Are you crazy?"

"Hold still, Martha," he said and wrestled the knife out of her hand. Martha quit struggling then and sobbed loudly. The detective reached into his pocket for his cell phone and hit speed dial.

"Are you all right? Do you need an ambulance?" he asked me.

"No, I'm fine," I said, shaking myself. I sat back on the sofa, breathing hard.

Detective Blanchard placed the call for backup while I caught my breath. I stared daggers at Martha as she sobbed loudly. And to think, I had felt sorry for her in her grief.

I looked at the detective. I owed him one. A big one.

Chapter Twenty

I was sitting at a corner table at the Center Street Cafe, waiting for Detective Blanchard. He came through the door, and his broad frame briefly blocked out the morning sun. I had invited him there for breakfast as a thank you for saving my life. It wasn't much, but it was all I had to offer him. That and I planned on baking him a pie later. The day before had been the first time I hadn't baked a pie every day since right before my husband's funeral. The day before the funeral, I had been tied up in knots with grief and realized that people would be coming to the house afterward, and I would need to serve them something. I baked sixteen pies that day, well into the early morning hours. I had needed something to keep myself busy, and that filled the bill.

I smiled at him as he took a seat across from me.

"Good morning," he said with a relaxed smile on his face. It was a nice change.

"Good morning, Detective Blanchard," I replied.

"Please, call me Alec," he said. This was the most personable I had seen him since we had met.

"Alec, I really just wanted to say thank you for saving my life," I said. "I know this isn't much of a thank you." I blushed at the absurdity of trying to thank someone for saving your life with breakfast.

He chuckled. "I've never gotten breakfast as a thank you before. It's unnecessary, but much appreciated."

"And I'm going to bake you one of my famous pies and bring it by later. I'm thinking apple blueberry. How does that sound?" I asked, glancing from my menu to him and back again. I was suddenly feeling shy for some reason.

"That sounds wonderful," he beamed. "The truth is, I was wondering when I would get to taste one of your pies. The talk all over town is that they're the best around."

"Really?" I said and felt myself go pink again. "I had no idea that I had a reputation."

"Indeed you do," he said with a grin and turned to his menu.

"How did you happen to come by my house at that moment? If you hadn't, I shudder to think what might have happened," I said and took a sip of my coffee. The coffee here at the café wasn't fancy, but it was caffeinated, and you had to respect that.

"I had my suspicions about Martha. I was coming by to talk to you. I wondered if, in your highly inappropriate investigations, you had heard anything that might prove I was right," he said, looking me in the eye. "I heard you screaming, and fortunately, your door was unlocked."

"What kind of suspicions? I swear I hadn't thought of her as a suspect at all, especially with her old and feeble act she always put on." I was still stunned that she was the murderer.

"She was there the morning of the crime, which honestly didn't mean a thing to me at the time. But it seemed that everyone I interviewed had had some contact with her afterward. It was odd. At first, I thought it was just because this is a small town, and also because she had seen Henry dead on the floor. Everyone seemed to want to comfort her, and I didn't think much of it. But the more I heard about her going to other people and asking questions, the more I thought there might be something there. I'm just sorry you came so close to being her second victim."

I nodded, taking this all in. "I guess it's good I'm not a detective then. I'm dumbfounded about the whole thing. So, did Martha tell all?" I asked. I wanted to make sure she didn't hold out on anything.

"She did. She's a bitter little lady," he said and chuckled. "I've seen a lot of things in my twenty-plus years of being a detective, but nothing like this. I really didn't want to believe it, but once I saw her with a rather large knife poised over you, there wasn't any denying it."

I sighed and sat back in my seat. "I'm just glad it's over. I feel bad that poor Henry had to die though."

"It's a shame. It always is when someone is murdered," he said and glanced at the menu. "I think I'm going to have the veggie omelet."

"I think I'll have the same," I said. He sat back, and we looked at each other in the eye. His were bright blue. Mine are green. He was a handsome man, and it wasn't lost on me. I was glad I was no longer public enemy number one to him, and I wondered if he was single. A twinge of guilt washed over me. I did not need a man. No one could replace my husband. We had been perfect together, and any relationship I might have started with someone else would only end in frustration when another man couldn't measure up to Thaddeus. Because no one could. It was impossible.

Still, the thought floated across my mind.

The End

Sneak Peek

Trick or Treat and Murder
A Freshly Baked Cozy Mystery, book 2

Chapter One

"No monsters are out tonight, Daddy shot them all last night," I sang to myself as I pulled up to the Halloween Bazaar. I had taken liberties with the song in honor of the season. I parked my car and got out. There were only two cars in the Methodist Church parking lot, and that surprised me. It was just after two o'clock in the afternoon, and I thought the place would be bustling with people decorating the place and getting ready for the kids to show up in their Halloween costumes.

The sky was overcast, and I hoped we wouldn't get rain. I got out of my car and opened the back car door, picking up the large envelope of vintage-inspired cardboard cutouts I was going to use to decorate my booth. I placed the envelope on the plastic-wrapped tray of candy apples and put that on top of the two boxes of pumpkin hand pies I had made for the event. The scent of cinnamon and cloves wafted up to me as I lifted the two boxes, and I slammed the car door shut with my hip. Fall was my favorite season, hands down. I loved pumpkin everything, and the fall foliage in Maine was breathtaking.

Diana Bowen's green SUV was parked near the entrance. She owned the flower shop where my friend Lucy Gray worked, and she was the bazaar organizer. Diana was nice enough, but she was one of those people that talked all the time and commandeered conversations. Let's just say, she got on my nerves occasionally.

I got to the door and reached for the knob, but the boxes were too wide. I tried to maneuver them so I could get to the doorknob, but that didn't work. Then I kicked the door with one boot-clad foot and immediately did the ouchy-wowie dance. Bad idea. I waited a minute to see if anyone would come to my rescue.

"I guess I have to do this myself," I muttered and gingerly set the boxes down on the concrete.

Opening the door, I placed my hip against it and bent to pick up the boxes. "There we go," I said to myself and headed into the empty hall.

I smiled. There were bales of yellow straw and piles of pumpkins strategically placed around the room. In one corner there was a painted wooden cutout of great big pumpkins and a scarecrow with a hole cut around the face so people could stick their heads through it and have their pictures taken. Red, gold, and orange fall leaves were scattered on the tabletops. Black and orange streamers hung from the ceiling, and there was a helium tank with bunches of black and orange balloons attached to it. A pile of unfilled balloons sat on the table next to the tank. Simple, festive, and sweet.

The walls were lined with booths draped in alternating orange and black plastic tablecloths with enough streamers to decorate each one lying on top, ready for the booth's occupant to get to work.

I had requested the booth near the front of the stage. The booth next to it was filled with fall flowers and trinkets that Diana sold in her shop, so I knew she had been busy. But where was she now?

"Hello?" I called out. No answer.

The boxes were getting heavy, and my arms were beginning to ache, so I headed to my booth and set them down on the table. Picking up my streamers, I dug in my purse for the tape I had brought along. Humming made me happy, and since I was alone, I indulged myself. Lucy said it was annoying, but what did she know?

The steamers were cute as could be after I had them lightly twisted and draped around the top and front of the booth. I stood back to make sure they were draped evenly. I smiled, satisfied with my work.

Next, I picked up the envelope of cutouts and worked on putting them on the front of the booth. The cutouts gave me a warm feeling, reminding me of my childhood when I went trick or treating back in Alabama. Kittens, ghosts, and a little witch surrounded by pumpkins scampered about on the cutouts. It only took a few minutes, and I was done. I stepped back again and surveyed my work. The cutouts were adorable, and I decided I was going to have the cutest booth at the bazaar.

With that done, I went around to the back of the booth and stepped through the opening that served as a door, and stopped. Someone was lying under the table of my booth. My first thought was, *well, that's an odd place to take a nap.* Then

I realized it was Diana. Her back was toward me, so I couldn't see her face, but I recognized her teased and dyed blond and brunette striped hair.

With my heart pounding in my chest, I whispered, "Diana?" She didn't make a move.

I looked around to see if there was anyone else in the hall. Where was the owner of the second car I'd seen in the parking lot?

I turned back to Diana. "Diana?" I said louder.

She still didn't move. I felt in my pocket for my phone and pulled it out. Diana was lying very still. Maybe she had fallen? Or had a heart attack?

I took three steps toward her. She still didn't move, and I was getting a serious case of the heebie-jeebies. I knelt and stretched my hand toward her, but I wasn't close enough. I scooted forward on my knees a few inches until I could touch the back of her neck. Her skin was cold as ice.

I jumped up and backpedaled until I was out the opening of the booth. My heart pounded in my chest, and I took a deep breath. "Oh, my gosh," I whispered. "Diana."

I dialed 911 and told the operator I thought there was a dead person at the Methodist Church recreation hall.

After taking my information, she asked, "Did you check for a pulse?"

"A pulse? No, she's really cold. I don't think there's a pulse," I said, biting my lip and keeping an eye on Diana. I didn't want her suddenly changing her mind about being dead.

"Is she breathing?" the operator asked.

"No. She's dead," I said, trying to keep my voice from cracking. My mind was churning, and I just wanted someone to show up and handle things for me.

"Are you certain?" she asked, sounding as if she were talking to a child.

"Listen, lady, the only thing I'm certain of is that today is Saturday. Can you please send an ambulance? Or a policeman?" I said. I tried not to sound rude, but I didn't want to touch Diana again, and since she still hadn't made a move or a sound, I was pretty sure she was still dead.

The operator sighed loudly. "Fine, I'll send the police and an ambulance. Don't you move. You wait right there for them," she ordered.

"Fine, I'll be right here," I said and clicked my phone off before she could say anything else.

Poor Diana, I thought.

I backed farther away from her body and shivered. I looked around at the still empty room. Why did I have to be the one that found her? Couldn't there have been at least one other witness somewhere nearby?

I wandered over to Diana's booth and took a look inside for something to do and to keep from having to look at her body. Diana had the prettiest nick-knacks at her flower shop. She had brought several fresh flower arrangements for the raffle that would happen later that evening. If the bazaar was still on.

Oh no, what if they canceled the Halloween bazaar?

Diana had put so much work into the bazaar. We were going to raise money to fund the community Thanksgiving dinner and buy coats for less fortunate children next month. It would be a shame if it were canceled. There was a bowl of candy corn in Diana's booth and the scent of cinnamon hung in the air. I stepped inside and kicked something.

What was that?

I knelt and reached under the table, pulling out a half-eaten candy apple. It was one of those cheap candy apples from the grocery store with the super sweet red coating and finely chopped peanuts on it. I tossed it back on the floor. The red sticky coating had melted in the warmth of the room and was stuck to my fingers. I reached for a tissue from the box on Diana's table and wiped my fingers. Gross. I ran around to the front of my booth and reached into my purse for hand sanitizer and squirted it onto my hands. Sirens filled the air, and I looked toward the door. Thank goodness.

Before anyone entered the building, I texted Lucy and told her to get over here, stat. She would be devastated. She had been close to Diana.

I heard the hall door swing open, and I turned around. Ellen Allen. Her green hair had been teased to stand on end, and her nose ring twinkled under the lights of the recreation hall. It wasn't a Halloween costume. Ellen always looked like that.

"Hey, Allie, I brought some cookies my mom baked for the bazaar. That witch Diana isn't around, is she? I don't want to run into *her*," she said and strode toward me with a huge platter of cookies stretched out toward me. She took long strides as she walked. Ellen was just over six feet tall, and she could cover some ground when she needed to.

I bit my bottom lip. Ellen had been fired by Diana a month earlier. Lucy told me it was because Diana had caught her stealing from the cash register. She would make a good murder suspect if foul play was involved in Diana's death. Not that I expected that, but you never know.

"Ellen? I have some really bad news," I said.

"Do you hear all those sirens? Sounds like they're getting closer," she said, furrowing her brow. She set the platter of cookies on my booth. "What bad news?"

"Diana's dead," I said as the sirens got louder.

Her eyebrows flew up, and I noticed a tiny diamond stud at the end of one of them. "What?"

"Dead. Diana is dead," I said. We both turned toward the door as the sirens stopped outside the building.

She turned back toward me. "Stop foolin' with me. I don't want to run into her, so I have to get going."

"I'm serious," I said and pointed over the side of my booth.

"Huh?" she said and leaned over the side to look. She was tall enough to see Diana without going around to the booth entrance in the back. "Wow. So she is. Did you kick her to make sure?" She looked at me with just a hint of a smile on her lips.

The hall door opened, and police officers Yancey Tucker and George Feeney walked through it.

"We heard there was a body?" Yancey asked.

"Yes, right over here," I said, pointing to the general area where Diana was lying. I wasn't getting close to her again.

Yancey stepped around the booth to the backside. He went into the booth and squatted down next to Diana's body.

I glanced over at Ellen.

"Tragic," she said with a smirk.

It was my turn for my eyebrows to fly up. I didn't expect her to cry about Diana being dead, but I thought she might show at least a little concern for Diana or her family.

"Hey, Allie?" George asked as he peered over the side of my booth and watched Yancey.

"Yes, George?"

"Didn't you discover Henry Hoffer's body last month?" he asked, looking at me.

"Uh, yeah, I guess I did," I said, narrowing my eyes at him. He had better not get any ideas about me being involved. I didn't do anything.

He stared at me without saying another word. I suddenly wanted to run away from that place. I felt bad about Diana, but I didn't want to be a suspect again. The stress of it all was more than I could take. Ellen smirked again, this time at my obvious discomfort.

The hall door opened again, and Detective Alec Blanchard walked through it, taking long strides across the room. His mouth formed a hard line when he caught sight of me.

"Allie," he said, nodding. He glanced at Ellen and then turned back to me.

I pointed over the side of my booth, and he leaned over just as Yancey popped up from his position on the floor. Detective Blanchard nearly jumped out of his skin and barely managed to suppress a girl-like scream.

Ellen giggled and turned away. I'd like to say I didn't laugh a little, but it would be a lie.

The detective straightened his tie and ignored us. He cleared his throat and looked at Yancey pointedly.

"Uh, sorry. Yeah, she's dead. No pulse, and her body's cold."
I could hear an ambulance with its siren blaring arrive.

"So, Allie, do you make it a habit of discovering dead bodies?" Detective Blanchard asked me, tilting his head.

"No," I said and shook my head. I had hoped we had developed enough familiarity after the last murder for him to not assume I might have had something to do with this one. I had bought him breakfast and made him an apple blueberry pie as thanks for saving my life, after all. It looked like I might be wrong.

You can buy Trick or Treat and Murder here:
https://www.amazon.com/
Trick-Treat-Murder-Freshly-Mystery-ebook/dp/
B01LWIWXRN/

If you enjoyed Apple Pie a la Murder, please consider leaving a review. Reviews help me to gain visibility on Amazon.

https://www.amazon.com/gp/product/B01KS3PYXQ

If you'd like updates on the newest books I'm writing, follow me on Amazon and Facebook:

https://www.facebook.com/
Kathleen-Suzette-Kate-Bell-authors-759206390932120/

https://www.amazon.com/Kathleen-Suzette/e/
B07B7D2S4W

Made in the USA
Columbia, SC
15 September 2022